TYLER'S PURSUIT

by
Elizabeth Galyen

PUBLISH
AMERICA

PublishAmerica
Baltimore

ISBN: 1-4241-1837-9
PUBLISHED BY PUBLISHAMERICA, LLLP
www.publishamerica.com
Baltimore

Printed in the United States of America

To: Lynda –
A great lady and the
one who exhibits to me the
meaning of "Best Friend".
I will never forget you!
Love,
Jamie
2006

Chapter One

Samantha and Todd's wedding couldn't have gone more smoothly. The church is absolutely beautiful and alive with all the decorating that has been done. Samantha is beaming as she and Todd retrace their steps as they walk back up the aisle to start their lives together as a married couple. Thank God, Samantha hasn't seen Tyler standing at the back of the church. He'd been able to duck out just before they turned to walk back up the aisle.

Tyler observes enough to know that the second chance he thought he might have had with Samantha has now vanished. He slowly walks to his car to drive back to Pittsburgh to start a new life for himself that he is now convinced will not include Samantha. His biggest regret was sending Samantha away at the hospital and not letting her make her own decision, whether to take a chance with him during his recuperation following the accident. But hindsight can't help him now and there's no point in pondering what ifs.

One Year Later

"Samantha, may I see you before you leave today?" George asks her over his phone intercom.

"Sure, George. I'll be there in just a few minutes," she replies pushing the intercom button.

George is Samantha's boss and has treated her like his daughter since the day she hired on. When she and Tyler were injured during their investigation into Courtney's murder a year and a half ago, he thought he might have lost her. They were both lucky enough though to have come through it without permanent damage. Every since then he's been a little over protective of her and isn't exactly thrilled that she and Todd are taking this skiing trip to Colorado. However, he'd never want Samantha to know it.

She finishes putting the last of her paperwork safely in the drawer, knowing full well that she won't be returning until after the holidays. She and Todd are spending their first anniversary away from their home in Palmetto, South Carolina and are flying to Steamboat, Colorado for a ski trip and to spend the holidays. This will be the first time for them both to leave the warmth of the south and head west where it will be cold and the snow will be flying. They have longed to try their hand at skiing again and see what it would be like to have snow for Christmas. Both sets of parents aren't pleased that they will be gone over the holidays, but understand they have to cut the apron strings and let them lead their own lives. They already celebrated Christmas with them earlier in the week, exchanged gifts and had a lovely dinner. They'd all said their goodbyes and wished them a great holiday.

Samantha takes one last look, turns and locks her office door before making her way across the hall to see George.

The door to George's office is open, so she walks in as he's hanging up the receiver. Had she known that he's been talking on the phone with Tyler she wouldn't be a happy camper. She doesn't know that George has kept in touch with him and has since their accident. It's been well over a year now since Tyler and Samantha went to the university to investigate Courtney's death. But it's been really tough for Tyler since the wedding and he hasn't been able to get Samantha out of his mind. There's nothing George can do but be there for him to lean on when needed. He still feels partly responsible for the whole mess that he and Samantha were in.

"Hi, Samantha. Are you all ready to leave?" he says, putting his conversation with Tyler aside.

"Yes." She smiles. "I just locked my door before I came over and I think everything is in order," she replies and sits down in the chair in front of George's desk.

"I just want a chance to wish you happy holidays before you leave. I saw Todd a few minutes ago and wished him the best also. He's so excited for the two of you to be getting away to enjoy the holidays. I can hardly believe that it's your first anniversary. Where has time gone?"

"Thanks George and happy holidays to you also. I know it seems like just yesterday we were planning the wedding." Looking down at her watch she replies, "George, I must get going. I'm meeting Todd back at the house to get the car packed, and then we're off to the airport."

George moves around his desk to give Samantha a big hug. "You two have a great time and please be careful. I don't want to hear of any broken bones that will lie either of you up. I'll need you coming back with both feet running when you return," he says, pointing his finger at her. "Now go on, get out of here."

Samantha gives George a hug in return and wishes him the best of the holidays. He's become a very important part of her life and knows that she can rely on him anytime anywhere.

Todd's packing the car as Samantha pulls into the driveway. "Need any help with that?" she asks, climbing out of the car.

"No, thanks, but there's still plenty left in the house to bring out," he says, drawing a deep breath after lifting the heavy suitcases into the trunk. Knowing full well that she's pushing the limit on what they will be allowed to take on the plane, he doesn't say anything to upset the beginning of their vacation.

"Great," she says. "I'll quickly change into something more comfortable for traveling and I'll be out momentarily."

It doesn't take her long to change and coming down to the kitchen she observes Todd raiding the refrigerator. "What are you looking for? I'm afraid you won't find anything in there to eat. Since we are going to be gone so long, I cleaned almost everything out."

"That's okay, I've just got the munchies. I need to get gas on the way to the airport anyway and I'll grab a snack there to tide me over. Flying first class, they'll have something for us during the flight out anyway. Are you ready?" he asks, closing the refrigerator door. "If we don't leave soon we're going to be behind schedule and you know how the airports are now with being there two hours before flights are to leave."

"Yup, I'll just double check to make sure I haven't missed anything. I see that you've gotten the rest of the things in the car while I was changing," she says, turning to make one last trip through the house.

"Everything's in. I'll wait for you in the car."

Chapter Two

Todd and Samantha's flight to Steamboat is uneventful. They're so excited that it seems like no time and they are here. Thankfully the flight was long enough that they fed the passengers and Todd got to eat.

"Passengers, please remain seated and fasten your seatbelts," the stewardess states over the microphone.

"Look down there Todd. The snow is beautiful," Samantha says, pointing out the airplane window as the airplane is descending towards the airport. There is so much snow on the evergreens that some of the branches are touching the ground. "I'm so excited I can hardly wait. It's been so long since I've seen mountains or snow. We are really going to have a great time, aren't we?"

"Samantha, we are going to have a blast, I promise. We've so looked forward to this vacation and it is much needed for us both. Nothing is going to get in our way."

"Ladies and gentlemen," the Captain says, "thank you all for traveling Northwest and hope you enjoy your stay. For you skiers it looks like there's plenty of snow."

"Oh Todd, I can't wait," she says again. "I know it's too late to ski now, but I'll be ready first thing in the morning. I know I haven't skied in a long time, but it shouldn't take long to get my ski legs back."

"Now calm down, Samantha. You have been so excited I can hardly keep you contained," he says, putting his arm around her shoulders and giving her a squeeze. "But I bet you fall down more times than I do!"

"Want to make a bet?" she asks, elbowing him in the ribs.

"Yes, I'll make you a bet!"

"Okay what are the stakes?"

"I'll bet you a new outfit for me that you fall first!"

"You are on. It's a bet then. That you fall more times than I do the first day. How's that?"

"Fine!" Samantha says. "The bet starts first thing we hit the slopes tomorrow."

The plane has landed and comes to a complete stop while the two of them have been making their wager.

"Samantha, have you picked up everything that we brought on board?" Todd asks, rising out of his seat and stepping into the aisle.

"Yes, I believe I have it all," she says, standing up and turning to step into the aisle after Todd. "Can you take this carry on for me, please? It's really heavy."

Taking the carry-on from her, he asks, "Hey, by the way, what's in it for me when I win the bet?"

"Ha!" she laughs, walking towards the exit. "There is no way that I'm going to let you win!"

They'd already decided to rent a car at the airport to use during their stay at Steamboat. As soon as their luggage is claimed they find the car rental counter to obtain their car. Everything goes smoothly and they're told where their car is located.

They find their car and they both approve. They'd requested an SUV to be able to maneuver the snow since neither one of them have driven in snow in years.

"Get in," Todd exclaims. "I can't wait to see the chalet we've rented."

"Me either," she says and smiles. "This is going to be a vacation we will never forget. I'm ready for some fun."

Todd's reached the turnoff that he'd been instructed by the renters to take to the chalet. Both he and Samantha are pretty much wiped out from the extremely long day, but are instantly brought out of their stupors when they see the chalet.

"Wow!" shouts Samantha ecstatically. "Todd, this is absolutely beautiful!"

"Awesome!" Todd says, turning into the driveway. He continues driving up the driveway and at the same time tries to take in the chalet and it's scenery.

"Just what we wanted," Samantha cries. "I only hope that everything holds true on the inside. Surely, it's just as wonderful there, too. I can't wait to get inside."

Turning off the ignition, Todd asks her if she wants to get the car unpacked now or check the place out first.

"I can't wait. Let's check it out first and then come back for our stuff."

Taking Samantha's arm to help her stay afoot in the deep snow, they head for the front door. Todd sweeps Samantha off her feet when they reach the front door. "Well, sweetheart, let's go inside."

"Todd, put me down!" she exclaims. "This isn't our honeymoon!"

He hands her the key to open the front door as he's still holding her and she kicks the door open with her feet.

"It's exactly as I'd envisioned, Todd," Samantha exclaims excitedly and sees the place seems to be immaculate. The living room, dining room, and kitchen are pretty much all one huge open space. The décor is done in deep burgundy and greens. The couch and loveseat are the same colors covered in plaids. The stone fireplace takes up one whole wall and is beautiful. The kitchen looks newly updated and very clean.

"Great, Samantha. Let's check out the rest of it."

"Fine, but will you please put me down first?"

Todd lets her feet hit the floor before he lets go of her completely and the two of them check out the rest of the chalet.

The chalet is basically located on one floor with a loft area for the master bedroom. Todd leads Samantha up the stairs to check the bedroom out. As they reach the top of the stairs Samantha is shocked at how beautifully it's decorated. There's a sleigh bed on the long wall covered with a multi-colored quilt and matching chest of drawers and dresser on either wall. Samantha walks over to open the door on the far wall and enters the master bath. It, too, is more than both of them fathomed.

"Wow!" Samantha says, taking in everything in the bathroom, including the Jacuzzi tub. "We could only dream of owning something like this. It sure isn't southern style, but it's absolutely awesome."

"We can dream, though, can't we? We can enjoy it to the fullest while we are here. Now, I'll race you back downstairs to unload the car. It's getting late and if we don't do it now we will both be too tired."

Samantha turns and tries to beat him to the stairs as her grabs her and pushes her down on the bed as to not let her get the jump on him.

"Not fair, you cheater!" Samantha exclaims, trying to regain her balance and hop off the bed.

Todd beats her to the car and is starting to take out the luggage when he hears her feet crunching the snow as she comes up behind him with a huge snowball. He turns just in time to get the full force of it straight to the face. He's without any hands for protection and hurriedly drops the suitcases to run after her as she's trying to gain distance between them. She doesn't get two steps before he grabs her by the arm and thrusts her down in the snow. Grabbing a handful of snow he rubs it on her face as she's trying to use her feet to kick his butt and wiggle free.

"Oh, no, you don't!" he shouts laughingly. "You're down for the count now."

"Todd, let me up," she cries. "I promise I won't do it again!"

"Why don't I believe you?" He stops her moving by trapping her arms over her head. In an instant he plants a kiss on her lips and she starts to melt. He loosens the grip on her arms and she wiggles free and puts both of them around his neck and pulls him closer.

She truly loves Todd and he's the best thing that's happened to her in a very long time. It'd taken her a long time to get over Tyler, but she now knows that everything happens for a reason and her reason is Todd.

She doesn't want to release her grip around Todd and their passion is heating up. Neither of them seems to care that they are still out in the elements and are lying in the snow. Todd's hand finds it's way up her jacket and manages to pull her shirt out of her slacks and reaches for her breast.

"Todd, I love you!" she says, not wanting him to stop.

That instant he picks up a handful of snow and manages to rub it on her bare stomach.

"No!" she shouts, breaking the romantic moment and trying to break free. "You set me up, didn't you?"

Laughing, he jumps up. "Yup, you asked for that! Now get up before you catch the death of pneumonia and let's get this luggage inside."

Chapter Three

Samantha is up before Todd the next morning. The flight must have worn him out. She's unpacked almost everything without even a stir from him. Breakfast is almost ready when he finally manages to make it down.

"Did the smell of breakfast wake you up sleepyhead?"

"I guess so, what time is it? How long have you been up?" he says, planting a kiss on her cheek.

"Oh about an hour. I've had time to unpack most of our things and cook breakfast."

"Great. I'm surprised you're not sitting by the front door ready to hit the slopes," he says, yawning.

"I can hardly wait. That's why I went ahead and started breakfast."

With breakfast over and dishes in the dishwasher, Samantha goes upstairs to dress for skiing. In no time she's back down and ready to go.

"Are our bets still on today, Samantha?" Todd asks, bending over to tie his boots.

"You bet it is and don't you forget it. I'm going to kick your butt on the slopes today."

"Ha! You just think you will. Grab your jacket and let's go. By the way, you really look sexy in that ski outfit," he says, eying her up one side and down the other.

"Thank you. Maybe this evening when we return I'll let you see what's under this outfit!" she says, sliding her body up against his.

A fresh blanket of snow fell overnight and Todd has a tough time staying on the road as they work their way out to the highway. Several times he finds himself veering off onto the side of the road but manages not to get stuck. Of course, he has Samantha making sure that she helps him navigate and lets him know every time he manages to get off the road.

"Samantha, what would the male population do without you women letting us know about every little mistake we make? Just hang in there and I'll get us there in one piece."

They arrive in downtown Steamboat in one piece as Todd thought they would and he doesn't hesitate in letting Samantha know that he'd gotten her there safely.

"Wow!" she exclaims, looking down the main street in Steamboat and all the little shops. I can do some serious shopping here!"

"Don't forget you live in a much warmer climate, Samantha. You won't need most of the clothes they sell here. That may be our only salvation to the checking account."

"But I can look, can't I? And besides, there seems to be several specialty shops that don't sell clothes. I'm sure there's a lot here to buy besides clothes."

"I don't stand a chance, do I, Samantha?" Todd asks, pulling into a vacant parking space. "I see a ski rental shop over there, let's go check it out. We'll also need to find someone that can give you a few lessons!"

"Lessons! I don't need any lessons. I can ski better than you any ole day."

They make their way to the shop to rent equipment but not until they've stopped and looked in the window of several shops on the way. He can tell he's not going to get out of Steamboat cheaply. Samantha's already told him which ones she wants to come back to, but right now they had skiing on their minds. She'll have plenty of time to hit the shops later.

The clerk at the equipment rental shop approaches them and asks if he can be of any help. "Hi, my names Justin. Interested in ski rental today?"

"Please," Todd says, "both of us need to be fitted."

Justin proceeds to ask both of them their sizes and leaves them momentarily to retrieve their skis. It's just a few minutes and he's back. "Try these and we'll see how they fit." Seeing how they maneuver the skis he can already tell they must be novices.

Both Samantha and Todd's skis are fine. They pay the rental fee, thank Justin for his help and can't wait to hit the slopes. Justin asks them if they have ski passes and upon finding out they haven't any, takes care of it for them and tells them where they are to go from here.

Once at the slopes they are both getting a little anxious. "Samantha, do you think you should have a refresher course before we go to the top? You know we can start on the bunny slope until you feel comfortable."

She agrees and the two of them hit the bunny slope until they have their ski legs and feel comfortable that they can hit the bigger slopes. They both agree that the day's bet won't start until they are off the bunny slope. It doesn't take either of them long to feel comfortable. It is just like riding a bicycle, you never forget.

"Are you ready?" Todd asks, knowing full well that he is going to win this bet after seeing how shaky she's been on the bunny slope.

"Let's go, I'm ready to have some fun. I can just see you now taking that first fall."

"A little over confident don't ya think!" he says as they take off their skis to make the trek over to the ski lift.

"We'll see who wins *this* bet," she says.

They put their skis back on and wait for their turn to ride the lift to the top.

Once at the top, Todd looks at Samantha to see if she's really ready for the slopes.

"Samantha, are you sure you are ready for this? You look a little scared," he asks, not liking the look on her face.

"No, I'm fine and I'm ready. And when you fall I'll meet you at the bottom," she says sarcastically.

"Funny, aren't you! The same goes for you."

Samantha pushes off with her poles and starts down before Todd. She smiles at him as she takes off and he waves. He pushes off right behind her and it isn't long before he catches her and smiles at her as he passes her up. She hollers something at him but he can't hear her.

He's skiing awfully fast for someone that hasn't skied in a long time, Samantha thinks to herself. The slope is quite crowded today, also. She sure hopes he knows what he's doing and doesn't get tangled up with someone. She's trying to maneuver the slope herself and lets Todd get out of her sight. This slope has more trees than she is prepared for and hopes Todd notices it, also, and is careful. She's thinking that maybe they're starting on a slope that's just a bit more difficult than their ability.

She still doesn't see Todd as she descends the slope, but is having a ball going so smoothly through the fresh powder that fell overnight that she can't wait to get to the bottom and do it again. She'd forgotten just how much she enjoys it.

Samantha reaches the bottom without even falling once. Looking around she realizes that she doesn't see Todd waiting for her at the bottom. After removing her skis she starts looking around for him. Within a few short minutes she realizes that he's not here.

"Hmm," she says, not realizing she's talking out loud. "Where could he have gone?" He wouldn't have just taken off without making sure that I'd made it down safely. She's getting a little worried when she hears sirens that seem to be coming her way. She notices that a snowmobile is coming down the slope at high speed and if he doesn't slow down he's going to plow into the crowd that is starting to congregate at the base of the slope. At the moment she's forgotten about Todd when she over hears a couple's conversation.

"I hope it's nothing too serious," the guy says.

"Me, too," the girl who appears to be with him says. "I hear sirens, though, so there must be injuries."

Samantha is getting nervous. "Miss, can you tell me what's going on?"

"I just heard that there's been an accident about half way up the ski run," the guy replies.

"Oh my God!" Samantha cries.

"Miss, are you okay?" the girl inquires. "You suddenly look very pale."

"My husband came down the run before me and I haven't been able to locate him since I hit bottom."

"Oh, I'm sure he's just gone to get some hot chocolate for you," she says, trying to reassure her.

"No, he wouldn't do that. We just arrived here last night and neither of us has skied in several years. He wouldn't have taken off without first making sure I made it down okay."

By now the crowd is growing larger and the siren that Samantha heard is approaching their location. The guy on the snowmobile she now notices is ski patrol and he's motioning the vehicle towards his location. The vehicle she hears is an ambulance. Her fears are escalating as she has yet to locate Todd.

"Ma'am," the lady Samantha's been talking with says, "you are really visibly shaken. Do you really think that it could be your husband who is injured?"

"*Yes!*" Samantha says with tears welling up in her eyes. "Where else could he be? If he'd gone to get us something to drink, he would have been back by now especially if he heard the siren and saw all of the people congregating. He would be worried about me and if I'd made it down okay."

"Scott, maybe we should try to talk with one of these guys and see if they can tell her anything."

"Maybe you're right. I hate to interrupt their rescue, but if it is indeed her husband she needs to know. Stepping closer to her he touches her arm. "Mam, I'm going to see what I can find out for you. Try to stay calm. It most likely isn't your husband at all, but some daredevil kids that ventured off and got themselves into trouble."

"My name's Samantha. Please, see what you can find out." She's getting more worried.

Scott approaches the guy that got off the snowmobile. "Sir, I hate to bother you right now, but there's a lady over here who can't locate her husband."

"Sir, we have an emergency up the run right now. You can talk with a policeman right over there," he says rather rudely as he points to the policeman who's trying to keep the gathering crowd calm. "He may be able to help her locate her husband."

"But, sir, I don't think you understand. Her husband came down the ski run ahead of her. She lost sight of him on her way down and when she reached the bottom he wasn't here. May I ask what's happened up the ski run?"

"Sir, where is this lady?" The ski patrolman asks Scott.

"Right over there." Scott points towards the crowd. "She's really shaken because she's worried that it's her husband that is injured."

"We do have a male that has been seriously injured," the patrolman whispers as they approach the two ladies. "But please don't say anything. I'll handle this. I want to ask her what her husband is wearing. That will determine whether it's him or not."

"Mam, I'm ski patrolman Hunter. This guy tells me that you are very worried about your husband."

"Yes, Mr. Hunter I am. Todd, my husband, came down the ski run before me. I lost sight of him on my way down and when I reached the bottom he wasn't waiting for me."

"Mam, can you describe what your husband is wearing?"

Samantha's shaking with worry at this point, but tries to describe what he is wearing. "It's pretty simple, really. He's wearing a navy blue, form-fitting ski outfit with red stripes down the sides. He's also wearing a red ski mask and goggles. Sir, do you think it is Todd?"

"Ma'am."

"Please call me Samantha. Is it my husband?" she rudely interrupts him.

"Samantha, I don't wish to alarm you, but your description of what your husband is wearing matches the clothing of our injured."

"Wait a minute, sir. Why couldn't my husband just tell you who he is? What has happened to him and how bad is he?"

As Samantha is trying to pull more information out of the patrolman, someone tries to reach him on his radio. "Rick, it's Jeremy here."

"Jeremy, we are doing our best to bring the injured down as soon as possible, but his vitals are worsening. We need a helicopter in here ASAP! We have to get him out of here within the next few minutes or he won't make it!"

"What?" Samantha cries.

At that moment Scott's wife, Tracie, puts her arm around Samantha to steady her. "Samantha, we'll stay right here with you. You won't be alone."

"Rick, I'll get one here ASAP. I'll make the call now and it should only take a few minutes to get one here. In the meantime do all you can to keep him comfortable."

Patrolman Hunter makes the call for the helicopter and is told its ETA. Rick told Jeremy the exact location of the injured and where they would be able to land the helicopter. Fortunately there is a clearing within fifty yards and Jeremy relays the information. Of course Jeremy knows his approximate position but Rick is more precise.

"Samantha, I need to get back up there," Jeremy says.

"I'm going with you," Samantha says.

"Sorry, ma'am, but that won't be possible." Looking at Scott, Jeremy says, "Can you take her to the hospital? We'll be taking him to Steamboat General."

"Sure, we'll stay with her and take her to the hospital."

"But I want to go with Jeremy," Samantha exclaims.

"Samantha, you can't do a thing up there. Let us get you to the hospital and you can be there when he arrives," Tracie says, hoping that she will agree.

Jeremy takes off immediately to return to the scene once he's told the ambulance driver that they are going to air lift Todd from the scene and that his services won't be needed after all. He knows very well that

Todd might not make it. When he came down a few minutes ago it didn't look good. He'd managed to avoid the question from Samantha on what is wrong with her husband. Her knowing that he'd have to be air lifted out was more than she needs to know right now. He only prays that Todd will make it. She seemed like a very nice young woman and a good-looking one at that.

Scott drives Tracie and Samantha to the hospital. It only takes about ten minutes so they are there before the helicopter arrives.

Upon entering the hospital, Samantha heads for the front desk. "My husband is being air lifted here, have they arrived yet?"

"No, ma'am, they haven't but they have radioed in and we're ready for them. Their E.T.A. is five minutes. You need to go to the emergency reception area and give them all the pertinent information on your husband."

"Thank you," Samantha says and Scott and Tracie lead her in that direction. They'd told her on the way over that they live just on the outskirts of Steamboat so they know the hospital well.

They no sooner arrive in the emergency area and two doors come crashing open and a gurney with a man on it is wheeled in.

"There's Todd!" Samantha cries and runs towards him, but as she starts to run a hand grabs her arm. Turning, she sees that it's Scott's.

"Samantha, they won't let you in there. Let them do their job and I'm sure as soon as they can tell you something they will."

"What if he doesn't make it?"

"You have to think positive and pray," Tracie says with tears in her eyes. She can hardly believe this is happening.

Samantha is crying uncontrollably now. "He has to make it. He has to! I love him so much."

"Samantha, is there anyone we can call for you?" Scott asks.

Samantha told them in the car where they were from and that they were here to enjoy the holidays and celebrate their one-year anniversary. "Both sets of parents are back in Palmetto."

"As soon as you furnish the desk nurse with Todd's information we'll get in touch with them."

"Thanks. Right now I need someone to do my thinking for me." She proceeds to the desk.

The whole time Samantha's giving the nurse the necessary information she's asking how soon she can see Todd or if the nurse can check on how he's doing. Just as she's about finished supplying his information the emergency room doctor comes out to find her.

"Mrs. Harrison," the doctor says, walking towards her assuming by her frightened look that she is indeed Mrs. Harrison. "Let's go in here, where we can have some privacy."

"Doctor, I'm Scott Hill and this is my wife, Tracie. This is Samantha Harrison, Todd Harrison's wife."

"I'm Dr. Blakely," he says, extending his arm to shake that of Scott.

"How's my husband?" Samantha asks, greatly concerned.

"Have a seat, Mrs. Harrison." Samantha sits and Tracie sits down beside her for moral support. "Your husband sustained serious head trauma, hitting that tree."

"What tree?" Samantha asks. "I don't even know what happened to Todd."

"From what information the ski patrol has been able to gather, your husband was unable to avoid a tree while skiing down the run. Other skiers observed him skiing too fast and he lost control. He then veered off the ski run and ran into the tree."

"Oh my god! Is he conscious?" Samantha asks, holding her head in her hands.

"No, he's not. Mrs. Harrison, I'm afraid his chances of pulling through this are slim. I suggest if there is anyone that you need to contact you do so as soon as possible. I don't see him making it through the night."

"Isn't there anything you can do for him Doctor?" At this point Samantha is shaking uncontrollably.

What Dr. Blakely isn't telling Samantha is that the blow to Todd's head crushed his skull and if he should pull through this he would be a vegetable. The best thing that could happen would be if God would take him now.

"No, Mrs. Harrison, there isn't. I'm afraid he's in God's hands now." He puts his right hand on Samantha's shoulder.

"Oh, no!" Samantha cries and leans into Tracie.

"I must get back in there now," Dr. Blakely says, moving away. "I'll let you know when and if there's any change."

"Can I be with him?" she asks as the doctor starts to walk away.

Turning, he says, "I think, under the circumstances, that can be arranged. Are you sure you can handle it?"

"I don't know, but I want to be with him. Scott, can you contact Todd's parents?" Samantha reaches into her purse to pull out the paper with both parents phone numbers on it and hands it to Tracie.

"Sure. You go on in and I'll try to reach them. Should I contact your parents also or let his parents do that?"

"Why don't you contact both sets, Mr. Hill? Then if they want to make connections after that they'll do so," Dr. Blakely says, leading Samantha towards the emergency room.

Chapter Four

Dr. Blakely knows Samantha isn't prepared for what she's about to see and luckily there are several nurses in ER to help her. The second she sees Todd just confirms what he already knew. She starts to crumble under his firm grip, but one of the nurses is close enough to help keep her on her feet.

"Mrs. Harrison, why don't you sit down here?" The doctor says, pointing to a chair in the corner. He and the nurse help her to the chair.

Samantha is as white as a sheet when she reaches the chair. "Oh, my God! Doctor I wasn't prepared for this." Todd's head was covered with white bandages and the part of his face you could see was covered with cuts, scrapes and blood. The blood had already seeped through the bandages.

Once she's had a chance to recover from the initial shock of seeing him, she rises out of the chair and starts towards the side of the gurney. "Mrs. Harrison are you sure your feet are under you enough to do this?" one of the nurses asks.

"Hm, Hm." She nods to the nurse. The nurse looks over at the doctor and he nods giving her permission to let Samantha go. Once at Todd's side she takes his hand into hers and starts to weep quietly. "Oh, Todd, I love you? You can't leave me yet; we've barely started our lives together." She then brings his hand to her face and rubs it on her cheek. As she does so the monitor hooked up to Todd flat lines.

Immediately, Dr. Blakely takes Samantha by the arm and says, "Mrs. Harrison, please step back. Nurse, get her out of here now!"

"Mrs. Harrison, will you come with me please?" the nurse says, trying to guide her out of the room as fast as she can.

"No!" Samantha screams. "I'm not leaving my husband!"

"Please, Mrs. Harrison!" Dr. Blakely insists as he reaches for the paddles to try to revive Todd.

They are all too busy now to notice that she's still standing in the corner of the room as they're trying to restart Todd's heart. Another doctor and nurse come in to assist and none of them pay any attention to her.

Shocking Todd's heart the first time doesn't help. Dr. Blakely clears again and nothing. He tries several more times and can't get it started. Finally he knows that it's no use and doesn't try again. "What time is it?" he asks one of the assisting nurses and she notes the time. "Damn!" he says, trying to catch his breath. "I was afraid this was going to happen. It is probably for the best knowing what kind of life he would have had, had he made it. Laying the paddles down, he wipes his forehead with his right forearm and turns to leave the room.

"Mrs. Harrison!" he exclaims, seeing her crouched in the corner and knows she's heard what he's just said.

"Why are you still in here?"

She was sobbing so hard she couldn't say a word. She had witnessed it all.

"Nurse!" he shouts. "What the hell is she doing in here? I thought I told you to get her out?"

"Sorry, Doctor," she says, turning to see Samantha. "I thought she did leave. We were so busy I didn't notice that she stayed."

The nurse crouches down in front of Samantha. "Mrs. Harrison, let's get you out of here."

"No," Samantha cries. "I want to be with my husband."

"Mrs. Harrison," Dr. Blakely says, "I'm so sorry." Looking at the nurse, he nods his head and says, "Let her stay with him a few minutes then get her out of here."

The nurse helps Samantha to her feet and guides her towards Todd. Once there, she lays her head near his shoulder and continues to cry. The nurse steps back for them to be alone.

Out in the hall, Dr. Blakely sees Tracie and walks over to her. She can tell by the look on his face that things aren't going too well.

"Dr. Blakely, how's Mr. Harrison?" she asks.

"I'm sorry, but he didn't make it. He expired a few minutes ago."

"But where is Mrs. Harrison?" she asks. "I thought she was in with him?"

"She is. He started to flat line and we thought we had her out, but apparently not. She saw it all."

"Oh my God!" Tracie says with tears welling up in her eyes. "She must be devastated!"

"Yes, I'm sure she is. I can't believe they didn't get her out. But everything started happening so fast no one noticed her in the corner. Has your husband been able to contact either set of parents?"

"I don't know. He hasn't come back yet. I'm assuming since he's still gone that he's reached someone."

"He's going to have to call them back immediately and let them know that Mr. Harrison didn't make it. His wife is going to need someone here with her and they should be told before they arrive."

"I'll go find him and have him call them back," Tracie says to Dr. Blakely. "I'm so sorry he didn't make it. But maybe the good Lord was doing him a favor if his condition couldn't have improved. I know Scott wouldn't want to live that way, no man would."

"I'm sure you're right, but at this point we'll have a hard time convincing Mrs. Harrison of that. I have to go now. I have another patient I need to see. Mrs. Harrison is spending a few moments with her husband. Will you and your husband be able to stay with her or do I need to have someone make other arrangements until their relatives arrive?"

"Scott and I will take her to our place when she's ready to go. We haven't any plans and won't leave her alone. I'm sure she'll want to go back to the motel to get a few things and that will be hard for her. I'll have Scott give the parents directions to our house when he calls them back. Thanks for everything you've done."

"If you need help in getting her to leave we have a clergyman. We can have him talk to her," he says and extends his hand to shake hers. "You two have been a great help to her. Not many people would have done what the two of you have done today."

"Thanks," Tracie says. "If needed I only hope someone would do the same for us."

Just as Dr. Blakely walks away Scott comes up behind Tracie. "How's Mr. Harrison?" he asks.

Tracie turns when she hears his voice and he can tell by the tears in Tracie's eyes that things aren't going so well. "He died a few minutes ago."

"Where's Mrs. Harrison now?"

"She was in with him when it happened." She sniffs. "They thought one of the nurses had made sure she was out, but things started happening so fast they didn't realize she never left the room."

"Oh my God, she must be devastated!"

"I'm sure she is. She's in with him now. The nurse will be bringing her out in a few minutes. Did you reach any of the parents?"

"Yes, I was able to reach his parents. They are probably calling her parents as we speak."

"Dr. Blakely says to have you call them back and tell them what's happened. He says it's better they know now so they can make arrangements accordingly. I told him that we'd take Samantha home with us till they get here. Is that okay with you?"

"Sure, by all means. We can't let her go back where they were staying, alone. I'll call his parents again right now and tell them. Tracie, I don't even know these people and I have to tell them their son has died!"

"I don't envy you, Scott, but I told the doctor we'd do it. He had another patient he had to see immediately."

"Great!" he says as he turns to go back and make the phone call.

Scott makes the second phone call to Todd's parents, explains what's happened and gives them their phone number. As he's coming down the hall towards Tracie, the nurse is following Samantha out. Tracie moves towards Samantha and puts her arms around her.

"What am I going to do without him?" she asks as Tracie takes her in her arms.

Scott reaches the two of them. "Samantha, I'm so sorry," he exclaims. "I've contacted Todd's parents. They will be here as soon as they can make flight arrangements. We're going to take you home with us and they will let you know what time they will be leaving Palmetto."

"What about my parents?" she asks, wiping tears from her cheek.

"Todd's parents are contacting them now. I'm sure as soon as they hear they will contact you at our place."

Chapter Five

It's really difficult for Samantha back at the motel. Tracie offers to go in with her, but she says no. She breaks down immediately upon seeing Todd's duffle bag in the corner and plops down on the bed. She'd given it to him as an early Christmas present to bring on the trip. He was very weight conscious and frequented the gym religiously. She knew that he needed a new one to replace the battered one he was carting to the gym and decided she didn't want to see him bringing it on the trip. But all of that seems so trivial to her now.

She'd like to stay awhile because she really doesn't have the desire or energy to make the effort to gather up her belongings and go with Scott and Tracie, but she also knows she doesn't want to be alone. Not wanting to make them wait, she pulls herself up off the bed and gathers up the things she thinks she'll need, but she finds it hard to see through her wet eyes. Tears are dripping off her face onto her ski jacket as she opens the dresser drawer.

She needs to make a decision whether to take just a few of her things, leave Todd's and keep the room or take everything with her. In an instant she decides to take a few of her things because her parents will need a room when they arrive and at this time of year the motel is probably filled to capacity.

At that precise moment she realizes that tomorrow is Christmas Eve and it would be their first anniversary. "Oh my God!" she cries and falls back down on the edge of the bed. She starts sobbing out of control and forgets all about Scott and Tracie waiting for her outside.

After it seems like an eternity since Samantha went in to the motel, Tracie tells Scott she thinks she needs to check on her.

"Maybe you should go check on her, Tracie. It has been awhile."

"I probably should have insisted that I go in with her in the first place," Tracie says as she opens the door. "But I wasn't sure what the right thing to do at the time was. I know she wants to be alone, but yet I'm worried about her."

"I'll wait here, you go ahead and check."

Tracie doesn't know the room number so she goes to the front desk to ask for it. The young lady at the front desk is reluctant to give it to her and wants to call the room and get permission from Samantha first. After dialing the room number and getting no answer she tells Tracie.

Worried, Tracie says, "Missus, I'm sorry, but Mrs. Harrison's husband just passed away this morning from a skiing accident. She came here to gather up her things to come stay with us and I'm worried about her. Is there any way you can let me into her room?"

"Let me check with my supervisor. I can't let you in without her permission, but I'm sure she'll get you in."

It only takes a couple minutes and the desk clerk and her supervisor are approaching the counter. "Hello, I'm Cindy's supervisor Sherry Clemons. I'm so sorry. I just heard about the skiing accident from a guest of ours that returned from the slopes. But I didn't know that it'd turned fatal."

"They did everything for him they could," Tracie says. "My husband and I don't even know them, but we just happened to be standing there when everything started happening and Mrs. Harrison was looking for her husband."

"Well, I'm sure she's grateful you were there. Come with me and let's go check on her."

Sherry knocks on the door to their room and Samantha doesn't respond. She knocks a second time and calls out her name, waits a few seconds and she still doesn't respond.

"I know she's in there," Tracie exclaims. "Samantha, it's Tracie. Will you please let me in? I'm worried about you." But Samantha doesn't answer.

"I don't like doing this, but I think we need to go in," Sherry says.

She unlocks the door and Tracie hurries in to find Samantha on the bed sobbing uncontrollably. "Oh, Samantha, I'm so sorry."

Samantha tells her that tomorrow would have been their first anniversary. They'd gotten married on Christmas Eve a year ago. They were here celebrating their first anniversary and Christmas.

Not knowing exactly what to do, Tracie looks at Sherry.

"Mrs. Harrison. I'm Sherry Clemons the motel supervisor. I'm so sorry about your husband. We'll do all we can to make your stay here a little easier. Why don't you gather a few of your belongings and go with Tracie. You can leave the rest of your things in here and we'll hold this room for you as long as you need it. Will your parents be arriving?"

Samantha manages a yes and tries to sit up and acknowledge Sherry. "Thank you." She sobs. "I'd really appreciate it. I have no idea at this point what I'll be doing, but I know my parents as well as his will need rooms when they arrive. "Can you accommodate them also?"

"Yes, we can. We always hold a few rooms even though we say we're filled to capacity. Just let me know when they will be arriving and we'll do what ever we can for them."

"Thank you very much," Samantha says.

Tracie thanks Sherry for helping her and Sherry returns downstairs to her office.

Tracie and Samantha finish putting Samantha's things together and they return to Scott.

It doesn't take Scott long to realize what's been keeping them. From the looks of Samantha, Tracie's had her hands full.

Chapter Six

Both sets of parents fly to Steamboat together and arrive on Christmas day. They'd tried to make flight arrangements for Christmas Eve but everything was booked. They hated for Samantha to be alone on Christmas Eve, but Samantha's parents talked directly with Scott and Tracie and they'd assured them they'd see her through it.

Scott goes to meet them all at the airport Christmas morning. Samantha is having a really rough time and Tracie doesn't think she is up to making the trip to the airport.

Samantha's given Scott descriptions of her parents so he'll know whom to look for when their flight arrives. He soon knows that he didn't need a description because when Samantha's mother walks into the terminal there is no denying she is Samantha's mom. She could pass for Samantha's twin, only a little older.

Walking up to her Scott greets them. "Hello Mr. and Mrs. Summers, I'm Scott Hill."

"Hi, Scott. Nice to meet you," Samantha's father says. "Where's Samantha?"

"She wasn't up to coming, which I'm sure you'll understand. This has really taken its toll on her and yesterday was really rough."

"I'm sure it was. We are so grateful for all you've done. Scott, I'd like for you to meet Todd's parents, Mr. and Mrs. Harrison," he says, turning to them.

"Nice to meet you," Scott says. "We've talked on the phone a few times. I'm so sorry about your son."

"Thank you," he says, quite somber. "It still seems like a nightmare."

"I'm sure it does. Samantha will be so glad all of you are here. We've done the best we can to get her through, but she needs you."

"We're all anxious to be with Samantha," her mother says. "Let's get our luggage and check on our rental car so we can see our daughter."

"I'll help Mrs. Summers get the luggage while you check on the rental car," Scott says to Mr. Summers. Then we'll all meet you out front and you can follow me back to the house."

When Samantha's parents walk through the front door at Scott and Tracie's Samantha runs into her father's arms.

"Honey, we are so sorry," her father says holding her tight. "We're here for you now," he says and starts crying with her.

Her mother is crying also and Samantha turns to her, asking, "Mom, why did he take Todd away from me?"

"Honey, I don't know," she says helplessly. "But we will get through this, we have to."

Todd's parents aren't far behind Samantha's and are coming through the front door. They, likewise, are devastated and each share a moment with Samantha.

Scott and Tracie both are very gracious hosts and have been lifesavers for Samantha. "Why don't all of you make yourselves at home," Tracie says. "I've prepared a meal and I'm sure none of you have eaten well since this all happened."

"Please don't go to any trouble for us," Mrs. Summers says.

"I have this turkey and someone needs to help us eat it," she says, trying to make small talk.

"It doesn't even feel like Christmas," Samantha says. "Scott, Tracie,

I'm so sorry I've ruined your Christmas."

"Don't think another thing about it, Samantha," Tracie says. "We are glad we are able to help. We don't have any children yet, so it's no big deal. We can celebrate our Christmas later."

Chapter Seven

Samantha and both sets of parents decide to have Todd's body flown back to Palmetto and not have a service in Steamboat. It takes a few days to make all of the arrangements but it works out and by the time they are all ready to go home Samantha is doing a lot better. They know it will be rough once she reaches Palmetto and home, but for now they think she will hold together. She is insistent on flying back on the same flight as the casket, and the parents will accompany her.

At the airport the parents say their goodbyes to Scott and Tracie and thank them again for taking care of Samantha. It is hard for Samantha to say goodbye. She will always have two friends in Steamboat if she ever wishes to visit again which she knows she probably will never do. Steamboat will always hold bad memories for her. Samantha tells them she will keep in touch with them through phone calls, e-mail and letters.

The flight back to Palmetto is a very somber one. Samantha spends most of her time staring out the plane window reflecting back on how all of this has happened. The parents talk amongst themselves and wish there is something they can do to help ease her heartache and loss, but know that time is the best healer of all. Hopefully once the services are over she'll get back to work and begin picking up the pieces of her life.

The plane lands on time in Palmetto and Samantha sees the hearse approach the side of the plane where it will pick up Todd's body. Drained at this point, all she can do is stare. She gathers up her belongings that she carried on and heads towards the front to exit the plane.

Once they've retrieved their luggage from baggage claim her father says,. "Samantha, why don't you ride home with your mother and I'll drive your SUV. Where is it parked?"

With only a blank look on her face she remarks, "It's in long term parking." She points in the general direction of its location as she's telling him where the car is and then reaches for the keys in her purse. Mr. and Mrs. Harrison are saying their goodbyes at the same time. They all know there is no need to stand in the airport and talk. They will be seeing more of each other in the very near future at Todd's service.

Mrs. Summers drives Samantha back to her place. Samantha's always loved her little cottage on the beach and once her and Todd were married they chose to keep it and make it their home. Todd loved the ocean almost as much as she and his apartment in Palmetto wasn't even close to the ocean. So he didn't renew his lease. They'd made the cottage their home.

"Mother, I'd like to stay alone tonight if that's alright with you," Samantha says somberly as she's inserting the key into the doorknob.

"Are you sure that's a good idea?" her mother asks.

"Right now, I don't know what's right, Mother, but I think I'd like some time alone."

"Okay, dear, just let me help you get your things unpacked and then I'll go."

"We'll just put the suitcases in the bedroom and I'll unpack them later. Right now, I'd just like to take a walk on the beach." It's still daylight and a little chilly out. After all it is December.

Once inside Samantha spots the Christmas tree standing on the side table in the sunroom. She and Todd decided on a small tree even though this was their first Christmas tree together. They knew they were going to be gone during the holidays and didn't want a big mess to clean up when they returned. They'd said there'd be many more Christmases to put up a large tree. She now wishes they'd gone ahead and put up a big one. That was what both of them really wanted in the first place.

Samantha's father isn't far behind and she hears the garage door open. "There's Todd.," she says automatically without thinking.

"Oh, honey," her mother says, walking over to her and putting her arms around her.

"Mom, how am I ever going to get through this? I miss him so much."

"Just one day at a time, sweetheart. That's all you can do."

Samantha's father comes through the door from the garage and lays the keys on the counter not knowing Samantha thought he was Todd. But walking into the kitchen he sees the look on Samantha's face and can surmise what she must have thought. "Honey I'm so sorry," he says.

"That's okay, Dad. I guess it's only natural I'd think it would be Todd. I just told Mom that I'd like to be alone tonight."

"Are you sure, honey? We can both stay if you'd like. I'd hate to think of you here alone."

"Thanks, but I'm going to have to learn to do this sometime and I might as well start now."

"You've always been very strong," her mother says. "If you need us, just promise you'll call."

"I will. Now, both of you must be exhausted. Why don't you head on home?"

They both give her a huge hug and tell her they'll call first thing in the morning. They'll have to start making arrangements then.

Once her parents are gone she changes into a pair of sweats, puts on her tennis shoes, a light jacket and heads for the beach. The pier isn't far and it's mostly deserted except for a couple late fishermen. When she reaches the end she sees a couple dolphins playing in the water. Leaning on the wooden railing of the pier she starts to reflect back on her short marriage to Todd. She remembers how supportive and understanding he was when she was going through her breakup with Tyler. He was there as a friend not pushing a relationship, but in time that's exactly what it turned into. She constantly saw him because like her he also worked at *The Tribune*, she as an investigative reporter and he in advertising. And George, he is like a father to her. George Chambliss is the Editor of *The Tribune*. He's always looking out for her best interests and doesn't like to see her unhappy. So he enjoys playing cupid. He'd gotten the two of them hooked up when he couldn't stand seeing her so unhappy. Samantha's like a daughter to him because he doesn't have any children of his own.

She suddenly remembers them walking on the beach the day she finally realized that it wasn't just friendship anymore. He'd been so patient with her healing process with Tyler and he'd told her he wanted more than friendship, but she just wasn't ready. But she'd done some soul searching and she was ready to admit to him the love she really had for him and that he deserved. On the beach that day, well over a year ago now, she expressed that love. She remembers how excited he'd been and the love they shared that day. She'll never forget the look in his eyes and the smile on his face when she told him.

"God, how could you take him from me?" she asks, staring out over the ocean with tears stinging her eyes. Her spirit had been crushed once again.

She didn't even realize that she'd walked back down the pier and was heading toward their cottage. Everything she was doing was like an out of body experience. She had no feelings whatsoever. Upon reaching the porch she sat in the porch swing and Tyler popped into her mind. She hadn't thought of him since he came to see her the week before their wedding a year ago, pleading to take him back. She wonders what he is doing now and if he's gotten married. Once in a while George would tell her he'd heard from him, but she wouldn't ask any questions. He was a closed subject she didn't want to discuss. She didn't know that George kept a close eye on her for Tyler. Even though Tyler knew she was marrying Todd he couldn't get her out of his mind. He hated himself so much for sending her away after he was stabbed. His consolation was hearing from George about her.

Swinging she suddenly realizes that she's thinking of Tyler, of all people. "What in the world's the matter with me?" she asks herself out loud. She's thinking of Tyler and her husband has just died. But she knows the answer to that question. She's just lost someone else that she loved so much. The two experiences are so far apart, but yet so closely related. Why has God dealt her two blows?

The phone rings and she stops the swing to get up and answer it. She hasn't any idea who it could be because no one should even know she's back in town. But she's wrong.

"Hello," she says, curious as to who's on the other end. She's in no mood to talk with anyone right now. She looks up at the clock to see how late it is. It's only about seven.

"Hi, sweetheart, it's George," he says.

"I know I recognize your voice."

"Honey, I'm so sorry about what happened to Todd. I'm still having a hard time believing it."

"Thanks," she says, sniffling. "I feel as if this can't be happening to me. Just a while ago I swear he was coming in from putting the car in the garage and it was my father. I knew that, but I was expecting him to come walking in."

"Are your parents with you?" he asks, concerned.

"No, I want to be alone. Besides I'm going to have to stay alone sooner or later so I thought I'd try it now. But you know what George?"

"What honey?"

"All of a sudden this little cottage seems like a mansion and I'm lost in it."

"It's going to take a while Samantha. Just give it time. Why don't you call your mother and have her come back out to stay with you?"

"I'll be okay," she says. "But thanks for your concern."

"Samantha, I don't want you to worry about returning to work until you are absolutely ready. Do you understand me?"

"Thanks, George. I don't know if I'll ever be ready. There are too many memories of Todd there."

"Just don't rush into making any decisions, give yourself time. I know you love your job at the paper and it may be good medicine for you to return as soon as possible to get your mind off things. But your department is covered until you return."

"I'm not even going to think about work right now. I have the funeral arrangements to make and the service to get through."

"I understand completely. I just knew that you'd be concerned about your work and I wanted to assure you not to worry and I wanted to extend my condolences. If there's anything at all I can do please call, otherwise, I'll let you go and I'll see you at the service."

What she doesn't know is he called Tyler in Pittsburgh and asked him to fill in during her absence. When he'd heard about Todd he immediately called to tell him and at the same time asked him to fill in. Tyler didn't hesitate in accepting. He'd do anything for George and of course Samantha. George just wonders what Samantha would think if she knew? God only knows he hopes she doesn't find out any time soon. She would absolutely kill him. He's hoping there's no reason that she would come to the office and run into him. They'd both really be in trouble then.

"Thanks for checking on me, George. I love you and I'll be seeing you soon."

"Love you, too, Samantha. You take care. Bye."

Samantha hangs up the phone and goes to sit back out on the swing. She isn't in any hurry to go to bed. In fact, she wasn't going to sleep in the bedroom even if she thought she could sleep. The bed would be empty without Todd.

Chapter Eight

It's dark and raining the next morning when Samantha's parents arrive to take her to make Todd's arrangements. Samantha is dressed in a pair of black slacks and a black sweater. She looks exactly like someone mourning over a loved one. She has her hair pulled back into a ponytail because she doesn't feel like messing with it this morning. She wonders why she should care anyway. She's feeling pretty numb this morning. She hasn't slept at all.

"You don't look like you got much sleep, Samantha," her mother says, shutting the door.

"I didn't," she says. "I was on the couch all night. I couldn't bring myself to go to bed, knowing Todd wouldn't be there with me."

"Why didn't you call? I'd have come back out and stayed with you."

"I know, but I couldn't. Can we just go and get this over with?" she asks, looking for her purse.

"I'm ready if you are," her mother says. "I'll drive."

"Fine. I don't think I have the energy."

They arrive at the funeral home promptly at ten a.m. as previously set. Samantha hesitates at the door. "Mother, I can't do this," she says, stopping outside the door with her legs shaking.

"I know this is isn't going to be easy. But you have to do it. We'll be right here with you."

As they enter the side door of the funeral home a nice middle-aged man greets them. He's new to the area and neither parent knows him. It would have been nice if Courtney's uncle still ran the funeral home. It would make it much easier working with someone you know, but this gentleman seems nice enough.

"Mrs. Harrison, I'm so sorry to hear about your husband's unfortunate accident and you have our condolences. Do you have any preferences on what you'd like to pick out?"

"No, sir, I don't," she says, wiping tears from her cheek. She's very uncomfortable and the smell in this place turns her stomach. She knows that somewhere in this funeral home is Todd. "Is there anyway I can see my husband?" she asks.

The funeral director is shocked at the request. It's not that he hasn't been asked this question before but he wasn't expecting it. "Sorry Mrs. Harrison. He isn't ready to be seen yet. We still have some work to do on him.

The thought of what Todd must look like right now just devastates her more and she breaks down.

"Samantha, are you going to be alright?" her father asks. "We can come back if it's too much for you right now."

"No, just give me a few moments to compose myself. Sir, may I use your ladies room?"

He directs her to the ladies lounge where she enters and sits down on the couch they have in the lounge. It's quite a while before she's composed enough to return. But she does so and finds her parents making small talk with the director.

"I think I'm ready," she says, looking at her mother. "I'm sorry."

"Think nothing of it, Mrs. Harrison. We understand completely." He hands her a booklet to look at. "Look over this and it'll give you some ideas of what you need to do."

Looking at the booklet, she has no idea where to begin. "Should we start with the casket first?" she asks.

"We can if you so choose," he says. "If you'll come with me I can show you the different ones we have to choose from."

Samantha can't believe that this is the way-picking out a casket is done. It's just like shopping. My God, she thinks it's horrible. She makes the process fast and simple just to get out of there. She picks out a beautiful cherry casket with a cream colored silk lining. She's sure it's what Todd would have liked.

The next idea she has in mind she doesn't know if it will go over so well with her parents. Looking at her parents she says,. "Mom, Dad, I'd like for the service to be at the ocean. That is where I'd pledged my love for Todd and the place we love the most. Looking next at the funeral director, she asks. "Is it possible?"

"Mrs. Harrison," he says. "Your idea is fine. And I understand why you'd like for the service to be there. But you have to realize it'll be January. The weather is pretty unpredictable."

"But you aren't saying it can't be done?" she asks.

"No, I'm not saying it can't be done. It's your decision. I must tell you though that it will be quite costly to do."

"I'm sure it will be, but I'm quite prepared for whatever it costs," she says and the thought of doing this for Todd makes her day a little brighter. She has to do this for him.

"Samantha, if this is what you want then we are behind you," her father states. "I only hope the weather cooperates."

Looking back at the director Samantha asks,. "What happens if it is raining on Monday?"

"That's up to you. You may have the service here or in the church of your choice. If you have it in the church we must notify them of your plans in order to be ready in case of inclement weather."

"Then we'll have the service here if it rains. I'm positive that it won't rain though. God wouldn't do that to Todd."

They have one more stop to make and that is at the florist. It seems just like yesterday that they'd ordered the flowers for the wedding and now a year later they are ordering them for Todd's funeral. A good friend of the family Janet Morgan runs the flower shop and Samantha is confidant that she'll do a good job. When Janet hears where the service will be held she's quite thrown back. "You know, Samantha, it can be quite windy this time of year. Do you know what flowers you are wanting?"

"No, I don't, not really. Do you have any suggestions?" she asks blankly.

Samantha knows she doesn't want to use red. It reminds her too much of Christmas and it's one she definitely wants to forget. "What do you suggest for this time of year?"

"We need to use a strong sturdy flower, let me think," she says, looking into the cooler.

"Roses and carnations are going to hold up the best right now. Neither of them will take the cold, but we can make it work. You might think about donations to some charity, rather than have flowers at the service. It'll be hard to place them in the sand and they won't hold up."

"We added that to the obituary that will be in the paper," Samantha says. "We made it in the form of a request in lieu of flowers."

"Then I think I can make an arrangement for the casket that Todd would have liked, and you, too, Samantha."

It doesn't take but a few minutes more and all of the funeral arrangements are complete. The only thing left is to get a hold of the pallbearers and Samantha and her mother plan to do that this evening.

Chapter Nine

Monday the day of the funeral is perfect. It's sunny, a little cool, but not as chilly as predicted. The family made it through New Years Eve and New Years Day. Samantha spent New Years Eve at home. It was rough, but she spent it alone. During the day she'd taken down the Christmas tree and the other decorations. She didn't want to face them after the service. On New Year's Day her parents came over and they watched old movies and looked at family pictures.

But today is going to be for Todd. The service is at ten a.m. and at nine o'clock her parents show up at the cottage. Samantha has it all nice and neat. Her mother and a few close family members had prepared a meal for after the service. Samantha wanted it there in their home where she felt most comfortable. Todd would have liked it, also. He'd want her as comfortable as possible. They'd kept the menu simple, so there wouldn't be much of a mess to clean up afterwards.

Likewise, the service is to be simple, also. The visitation was quite lengthy, but they think there will be a lot less people at the service with it being held outside. Much to their surprise, the people keep coming.

Luckily, they'd set up more chairs than they thought they would ever use. Samantha is amazed at the people who are present. Evidently, they don't care about the weather. They just want to pay tribute to Todd.

Samantha sits in the front row flanked by both sets of parents. Todd was an only child like herself, so there isn't anyone else in the front row. The rest of the relatives are seated in the rows behind.

When the service begins the sun is shining brightly on the cherry casket. Samantha's holding up quite well until Nicholas, a longtime neighborhood friend of Todd's starts singing Amazing Grace and she loses it. She doesn't care though; she just lets the tears fall as she listens to Nicholas. He has such an amazing voice. He's sung at many weddings and funerals around town.

After the minister of Todd's church finishes with the service it's time for the eulogy. What even her parents don't know is that she's decided she's going to do it. It's the last thing she can do for Todd. As she approaches the podium that's set up on the sand she hears the whispers behind her. She knows that they all are wondering how in the world she will get through this.

"First I'd like to thank all of you for being here to say goodbye to Todd. Now I have my own goodbye to him."

"Most of you have known Todd for many years and many of you for more years than myself. We were not only friends in school but also at work and we use to pull antics on each other quite frequently. It was more like a brother, sister relationship. Todd, you were with me in good times and bad. It was my bad times that I love you the most. Not more than a year ago, you were there for me with unconditional love as a friend not yet as my husband. You spent many nights comforting me when my heart was breaking. I told you my inner most thoughts and you never gave me your opinion. You were there to listen and to comfort me. Even though you may have thought I wasn't taking my best interests at heart you let me make my own decisions, right or wrong."

"It took me a while to realize that it was the love you had for me even though I never let you in my heart. You once told me that it took all your will power not to let me know how you really felt. But lucky for me I realized it before it was too late. I never thought I could love again, but you showed me that I could. Todd, it was right here in this very place on the beach that I told you how I really felt and you told me you thought you'd never hear me say it. You waited patiently for me Todd and I will patiently wait till we meet again. I loved you then, I love you now and I will love you forever."

There isn't a dry eye on the beach when she finishes. She walks back to her seat between her parents and they too have tears.

"That was beautiful honey," her mother says.

"Thanks. I feel that he was really here with me and heard every word I said."

"I'm sure he was and he did hear you."

The minister finishes with a prayer then says a few words to Samantha before she gets up to approach the casket for the last time. She's elected to say her final goodbye here rather than at the cemetery. It is only fitting to be done here. The cemetery crew will take care of the burial and she will visit the grave later. Once she's said her final goodbye she takes a rose from the casket to keep and she walks with her parents up the aisle.

Everyone pays their respects one last time to Samantha and offer their help if she needs it. She's very grateful to all of them and everyone leaves except the ones that are coming over to the house afterwards. At least she thought everyone left. As she turns to say something to her aunt she spots George talking with someone who has his back to her. She thinks she recognizes who it is but she can't believe it would be him. As she's staring at his back he turns around and she gasps. It's Tyler.

Tyler sees her glancing over at him and he walks over to her. "Hello Samantha. I just wanted to come and pay my respects. George called me after the accident and I had him let me know when the services were. Samantha I'm not here to upset you. I only came as a friend. George thought it would be okay for me to come."

"Oh he did, did he?" she says, trying not to break down again. "Well, I think this time George was wrong."

"I'm sorry, Samantha. I wouldn't upset you for the world and you know that."

"Yes, I do know that, Tyler. But now isn't the time for you to be here. I'm paying my last respects to my husband and my former boyfriend shows up. How must that look?"

"I'll leave right now then. Samantha, I am truly sorry for what has happened. If at anytime you feel that you want to talk, would you let George know?" he says and rubs her arm with his hand.

"I can't see that happening anytime soon." She walks away with the feel of his hand still resting on her arm. Damn, why did his touch do that to me? She rubs her arm.

Tyler walks back over to where George is still standing. "George, I think it best if I leave now.

"I'm sorry, what's happened?" he asks, not knowing Samantha didn't appreciate his being here.

"Samantha wasn't exactly excited to see me. I've upset her and I think it's best if I leave."

"Sure, let's go. Does she have any idea at all that you are working in her absence?"

"No, I'm quite sure she doesn't. And for your sake I hope she doesn't find out. "Give me a minute, Tyler. I'd like to let Samantha know I won't be at the house later."

"Fine, I'll just meet you at your car then. Give me your keys," he says, holding his hand out for them. He then walks to the car thinking about how he's upset her.

George walks over where Samantha's with her parents. "Samantha, may I speak to you a moment please?"

"Sure, George, let's walk over here," she says and points to the chairs.

"Samantha, I'm so sorry about Tyler being here. Had I known it'd make you this upset I wouldn't have advised him to come. Please accept my apology."

"George, you know you are one of my dearest friends and most of the time you have my best interests at heart. But what were you thinking when you ask him to come?"

"I honestly didn't think you would mind. I know you don't hate him, Samantha. And I know how he feels about you. I thought he would be a little comfort to you."

"I'm getting all the comfort I need from my family and friends. Don't worry about it George, I'll be okay. It's going to take time, a lot of time but I'm strong and I will get through this."

"I know you will Samantha, and again I apologize."

"Okay George, you're forgiven this time. But don't disappoint me again. By the way where did Tyler disappear to?" she asks, peering over George's shoulder.

"He took the keys and went to the car. He thought it best if he got out of here a.s.a.p."

"George, if you have a minute I'd like to tell you something."

"Sure, Tyler can wait for me a few minutes."

"I haven't even discussed this with my parents yet, but I'd like to take a leave of absence from work if that's okay with you? Do you think you can get along without me for a couple months or so?"

"Samantha I knew you'd want a little time off, but I never dreamed it'd be that long. I thought you'd want to jump right back in to keep your mind off things."

"George your right, that would have been me, but I want to do some traveling. Todd and I wanted to travel whenever time permitted and now that he's gone I'd like to visit some of the places anyway. It would give me some time to heal and maybe when I come back I'll be ready to jump right in."

"Sure you can have the time off. You have a lot of vacation time stored up anyway, don't you?"

"Yes, I do. Will there be a problem in getting someone to cover for me that length of time?" she asks. "Maybe Lee can take over my load." Lee is another worker at *The Tribune* and a good friend of Samantha's.

"Ah, no, I don't think that will be a problem at all. I'll see what Lee's working on and see if he can help fill in for you," he says, hoping she doesn't find out from somebody else before she leaves that he'd called Tyler down to take over her position. Now he only hopes Tyler can stay a while longer and cover for her. He knows Tyler loves it here, but he doesn't know if they can do without him in Pittsburgh for that lengthy of a period.

"Thanks, George," she says somberly. "I really miss him and it isn't going to be easy going without him, but it's something I want to do in his memory."

"How soon do you plan on leaving?" he asks, hoping she'll say soon. The sooner she leaves town the better his chances are she won't find out Tyler's working for her.

"Probably in about another week or so. I've got so much legal paperwork to do for Todd and I don't know exactly how long it will take."

"If you get a chance give me a call before you leave will you? I want to make sure my girl's doing okay."

"Sure. I wouldn't leave without checking in and you know it," she says, smiling.

"Now I must get to the house. I see Mom and Dad are ready to go. Are you coming by the house?"

"No, I don't believe so. Since Tyler's in town I think I'd better entertain him. You take care. I love you and I'll talk with you before you leave town." He leans down, gives her a kiss on the cheek and gets up to leave.

"Love you, too, and thanks for being such a good friend," she says, smiling up at him.

Chapter Ten

It took a little longer than she thought to take care of all the legal paperwork she needed to get done for Todd. January seems to have flown by and she hasn't had time to get away like she planned, but she's finally leaving Saturday. She just wants to make sure she's out of Palmetto by Valentine's Day which is the following Monday. She's flying out Saturday morning to Hawaii. Hawaii's one of the places she and Todd wanted to visit on their travels and since its still wintertime she wants to go someplace warmer.

Samantha picks up the phone to call George at *The Tribune*. She'd promised him she'd contact him before she left town and she hasn't had time to do so till now.

"Chambliss here," he says, picking up the receiver.

"Hello, George, it's Samantha."

"How are you, dear? It's been a long time since we've talked. I thought you'd have left town long before now. In fact, Lee was asking me about you just yesterday and wanting to know how soon you'd be back to work."

"I'm sorry, George. I should have gotten in touch with you sooner, but with so much legal work to handle I was a little consumed. How is Lee, anyway? Is he doing a good job covering for me?"

Taking a big gulp, George says, "Everything is going just fine. He's busier than a one-armed paper hanger, but he's managing." He'd forgotten he'd told her at the funeral that he'd ask Lee to cover for her just so she wouldn't know Tyler was covering. Her asking the question now throws him a little.

"I knew he could do it. I'll owe him big time when I return to work."

Just then, Tyler comes leaning into George's office to ask him a question, not knowing whom he's talking to. "George, do you have a minute, I need your advice?" Tyler doesn't know that George is on the phone with Samantha.

George motions with his hand for him to come in and have a seat. Covering the phone with his hand he says, "Have a seat, I'll be with you in a minute." But George isn't aware that as he says this to Tyler he doesn't have his hand completely covering the receiver.

Tyler has a seat in the chair in front of George's desk and waits.

"I'm sorry, Samantha, where were we?" he asks, forgetting their conversation.

"George, did I call at a bad time? Is someone in your office?" she asks, hearing the voice, but not quite able to put a face to it.

"No, no, you're fine," he says, giving Tyler a funny look and rubbing his forehead, feeling the pressure. "Now back to where we left off. Yes, you are going to be indebted to Lee for a long time and he plans on collecting when you return."

"I'll think of something nice to do for him," she says, still trying to place that voice. She knows she should recognize it, but she hadn't heard him well enough to.

"May I ask where you are going, Samantha? Or is that none of my business?"

By now, Tyler is sitting up, putting his elbows on his knees. He knows George is talking to Samantha. His heart is starting to beat faster. He still hasn't gotten over her and doesn't think he ever will. He's hoping she's calling to tell George she's returning to work, but since George just asked her where she's going, he realizes she's not.

"I'm flying to Hawaii bright and early Saturday morning."

"What!" George shouts.

"Yes, Hawaii. It's one of the places Todd and I wanted to visit and since it's the middle of winter in most of the places we wanted to visit, I thought I'd go where it's warm and soak up some sun."

Tyler gets the gist of their conversation and his heart sinks. It means she won't be returning to work in the near future. He was hoping to be back at his job in Pittsburgh by now, but it sounds as if it won't be anytime soon. The thought of running into her is out of the question.

"How long are you going to be gone?" George asks, staring across his desk into Tyler's eyes. He's aware Tyler doesn't like what he's hearing. He wishes he hadn't motioned for him to come in and have a seat. He would rather have dealt with this after he'd had time to think of how to tell him. With him sitting here, it puts a strain on his conversation with Samantha.

"I'm planning on a month. I know that's too long for Lee to cover, but do you think you could hire a temp? I'm just not ready to return to work, George."

"Another month!" he exclaims, shocked. "I'm sorry, Samantha, I just thought you'd be back by now. Honey, you take all the time you need. We'll put our heads together here and come up with something."

George opens his middle desk drawer and pulls out a sheet of paper. Samantha's about to give him all the particulars of where she's staying and a phone number to get in touch with her if need be. "Do you need me to check in from time to time? I'll have my cell phone with me."

"No, that won't be necessary," George says, finishing up with the information she's given him. You just go and have a good time. Just let me know when you're back in Palmetto and when you'll be ready to return to work. As of now, consider yourself on leave of absence."

"I love you, George, and thanks a bunch!" she says, wiping a tear away. He's been so good to her and she feels bad leaving him in a tough spot.

"You have a great time, but be careful," he says, looking at Tyler who has his head resting in his hands.

"Thanks. I'll send you a postcard! Bye." She hangs up.

"What in the hell is going on, George?" Tyler asks, leaning back in his chair and crossing his legs.

"Tyler, I'm sorry. I shouldn't have had you come in while I was talking with Samantha on the phone. As I'm sure you heard, she's leaving on Saturday.

"You still love her don't you, Tyler?" George asks, leaning back in his chair.

"You damn well know I still love her, George! So I guess you want me to stay and cover for her for another month?" he asks, sighing.

"Would you mind staying? I can sure use you. If you can't or won't I understand perfectly," George says, leaving his chair and heading to his credenza where his little refrigerator is to retrieve cold drinks for both of them.

"George, you know I love it here in Palmetto. It sure beats the winter in Pittsburgh. I'll make a few calls to my office and clear it with them, then get back to you. I only wish if I'm staying here that Samantha would be here, also."

"Sorry, but if she were here I wouldn't need you," George says jokingly and hands him a cold drink.

"Thanks," Tyler says, accepting the drink and the comment.

"Now what was it you were wanting when you came in here?" George asks, taking a drink.

"That's kinda of ironic," he says, smiling. "I was just wondering if you'd heard from Sam and when she'd be coming back. I got my answer, didn't I, and I didn't even have to ask."

"Yes, I guess you did. Are you going to be alright?" George asks, remembering he always called her Sam, short for Samantha. She always loved him calling her that. No one else ever did but him.

"I'd be better if you'd tell me where she's going," he says, prying a little and hoping George will relent the information.

"Sorry, Tyler, no can do. I won't betray Samantha. Now get on out of here, I have work to do and so do you!" he says, making a shooing motion with his hand.

Chapter Eleven

Samantha and her mother arrive at the airport two hours before her flight is to leave as requested by the airlines. She's packed enough clothes that you'd think she's never intending to return to Palmetto.

"Samantha, you'll be lucky if you meet the luggage requirements," her mother says, dragging the suitcase to the check-in counter. "This thing weighs a ton. What's in here anyway—bricks?"

"No, but I did bring a few books to read. I figure I'll have plenty of time on the long flight over and also while I'm basking on the beach," she says, smiling at her mother.

"No wonder it's so heavy then!" she exclaims. "I'm just glad you'll be relaxed enough to do some reading. I sure wish I was going with you."

"Not this time, I'll be fine. I think some time away from here will do me a lot of good."

"Are you sure you don't want me to wait with you?" her mother asks, knowing she has a while to wait for the plane.

"No. As soon as I'm all checked in you can head back into town. I'll take a walk around the terminal, get a bite to eat and maybe read a little."

Her check-in went smoothly even though the stewardess at the counter had a hard time lifting her suitcase. "Are you leaving for good?" she asks, smiling.

A few minutes later she and her mother are walking to the exit closest to where they parked.

"Be careful, Samantha, and please call," her mother says, tearing up. "Your father and I are going to be worried about you."

"I know, but try not to. I want to try and put this all behind me. I'll be fine and I'll check in weekly. Take care of Dad while I'm gone and I'll talk to you soon," she says and puts her arms around her to give her a hug.

"We love you and have a good time," she says, hugging her back, trying not to cry. Samantha has always been very strong. They both know she will be fine or they would have tried harder to talk her out of going on this trip.

Her mother heads for the parking lot as Samantha's waving at her. Looking back, her mother waves, also.

Samantha makes her way around the airport, checking out all of the shops and even picks up another book that she can't resist. Knowing they don't feed you much during the flights now, she also picks up some snacks and stashes them in her already stuffed carry-on bag she's pulling behind her.

Looking at her watch, she decides to find the nearest monitor to see if her flight is leaving on its scheduled time. Seeing that it is, she only has about thirty minutes before the first boarding is called, so she heads for gate 24 where her flight is leaving. She still has to go through that final inspection of handbag and shoes, etcetera. She can't believe they make you take your shoes off for inspection. What's this world come to?

Once aboard the plane, Samantha finds her assigned seat, which is, as she'd hoped, a window seat. It's still a few minutes before take-off and the seat next to here is not filled. Looking around, the flight is about two-thirds full. She thinks to herself she'd be just as happy not to have anyone sitting next to her. But her luck soon runs out. A man looking to be in his mid-thirties, approximately six feet tall, blonde hair, dark complected, and seemingly well-built reaches above the seat to put a duffle bag in the overhead compartment.

"Hello," he says, sitting down beside her and notices she's quite striking. She seems to be in her early-thirties with shoulder length, light brown hair, dressed in a pair of khaki slacks, a black short-sleeved blouse and sandals. "I believe this is my assigned seat."

"Hi," she responds back.

"Where is your destination?" he asks.

"I'm taking it all the way to Hawaii," she says, crossing her legs to get a little more comfortable.

"Same here," he says, pulling down the tray in front of him to place his laptop on. "Which island?"

"Oahu," she says, seeing his blue eyes for the first time.

"Same here," he says, noticing the wedding band on her finger. "Meeting your husband there?"

"What?" she asks, wondering how he knows she's married, then looks down and sees her wedding band. "No, I'm not. I'm recently widowed."

"I'm sorry," he says, genuinely sympathetic. "May I be polite and introduce myself. I'm Brian Shepard," and he extends his hand to shake hers.

"And I'm Samantha from Palmetto. Are you from Palmetto?"

"No, I live in New York. I've been in Palmetto, visiting my parents. They retired down here a couple years ago. I come down once or twice a year to check up on them. I'm going to Hawaii for a convention. The company I work for has their convention there every year. Not a bad place to go every year for a convention. This is only my second year and I didn't get to sightsee much last year. It was mostly work and no play, but this year I'm not a rookie anymore and I'm going to do more sightseeing."

"Wow, sounds like a great company to work for. What kind of work do you do?"

"I'm in media sales. Are you employed?" he asks, wanting to get to know more about her.

"Yes, I am, but right now I'm on an extended leave. I'm an investigative reporter for *The Carolina Tribune* in Palmetto."

"I've read it. Good paper."

"Thanks," she says. "My husband worked for them, also."

Without seeming to pry, he asks,, "May I ask what happened to your husband? Was he ill long?"

"Ladies and gentlemen, please fasten your seatbelts," the stewardess says over the speaker system.

"I guess we are about to take off," Brian says. "Are you afraid of flying?"

"No," Samantha says, fastening her seatbelt. "I've flown several times before."

"I believe you were just about to tell me what happened to your husband, when the stewardess interrupted us."

"He was killed in a skiing accident," she says sadly. "We were in Colorado, celebrating our first anniversary and Christmas."

"He's the one I read about in the paper."

"In New York?" she exclaims.

"No. I was going through a stack of my parents papers here and just happened to see it."

Both Samantha and Brian settle in for the long flight to Hawaii. Samantha pulls her glasses and book out of her carry-on and Brian opens his laptop.

"Do you read much?" he asks her. "Or are you just passing the time?"

"Actually I do read a lot," she remarks. "It's my way of relaxing. At home I sit out on my back porch in my porch swing and read as much as I can. I love the breezes I get from the ocean. But, of course, it's much cooler now and I don't get to sit out as much as I'd like, but it won't be long 'til I can start up again," she says as she notices he's pulled some papers from his briefcase. "If you have some work to do, I'll shut up and let you work."

"I'm just going to crunch some sales numbers to pass the time, that's all," he says, punching figures into his laptop.

"What part of media are you in?" Samantha inquires again with her book in her lap. She doesn't know why, but she'd rather ask him more questions right now than read.

"Sales," he replies. "Ad sales."

"Do you enjoy ad sales?" she asks.

"Yes, I do. I've been doing this for about five years now and I enjoy the people. I'm not crazy about all the traveling, but it goes with the territory. You get used to it after a while."

"Are most of your clients in New York City, then?"

"The biggest number of my clients are in the city, but I do cover a few south of the city," he says as he's wondering why she's so inquisitive. He's rather impressed that she really seems interested and he always loves to talk about his work.

"I'll bet you cover a lot of miles in a week."

"That's an understatement," he says and laughs. "I feel like I pass myself on the road by the end of the week."

"You said you are an investigative reporter, correct?" he asks, changing the subject and wanting to find out more about her.

"Right. I've worked for *The Carolina Tribune* just a few years," she says, looking into those blue eyes again.

"Have you been fortunate enough to work on any exciting cases yet?"

"I haven't had any in the last year or so, but Palmetto is rather a calm little city. Even with the tourist season it's pretty tame. The tourists are too happy to be there to cause too much trouble. I did have a former high school friend murdered a while back, though, and I worked on the case," she states, wondering if she really wants to get into this with him right now or with anyone ever.

"Oh, really! Did you actually get to help solve the case or did you just do the reporting?" he asks, quite interested.

"We ended up breaking the case, but not before we got ourselves in over our heads."

"Sounds exciting. Tell me more. I've got plenty of time to hear it. You said we. Was someone working on the case with you?" he asks, shifting in his seat to look more directly at her.

"Yes. My boss thought it might be a good idea to bring another investigative reporter down from Pittsburgh to help me on the case."

"You don't sound like you enjoyed that much. Do you prefer to work alone?"

"George, thought I couldn't keep myself out of trouble and that I needed a watchdog," she says sarcastically.

"And did you?"

"Did I what?"

"Keep yourself out of trouble?" he asks, laughing. Somehow he can tell by her tone that she couldn't.

"Tyler is the name of the guy who George brought in to help me. And, no, neither one of us stayed out of trouble."

"Tell me more, Samantha. This sounds exciting," Brian says, closing his laptop. He wants to hear this story and his number crunching can wait.

"It's a long story, so I'll try to keep it as short as I can, okay?"

"Tell it however you'd like. I'm all ears."

"Tyler and I found out as much as we could about Courtney, that's her name, from her parents, co-workers at the library, and friends. Tyler came to the conclusion that she had a split personality, because some things about her didn't add up. We even went so far as to visit the university that she attended to find out more about her. There, we found out that Tyler was right. She lived a very introverted life in Palmetto, but while at the university she was quite the extrovert."

"How?" Brian asks.

"It seems she had a boyfriend in college and she was still seeing him," Samantha says.

"Big deal! Don't all girls?" Brian asks, shrugging his shoulders.

"Not Courtney. And certainly not the boy she was going with!" Samantha exclaims, and now she really isn't sure she wants to continue on.

"What's wrong?" Brian asks, seeing the look on Samantha's face.

"It was my boyfriend."

"Your boyfriend. Go on, this is really getting interesting."

"I'm not sure I want to. Some of this is very painful. Maybe I shouldn't have started this at all."

"Then don't say any more if you don't want to." Brian says, resting his hand on her arm.

"No, I'll be all right." For some reason she really wants to tell him the story, but he's a complete stranger and she doesn't understand why.

"Jacob Benzing and I were lovers and all of a sudden, for no reason, he stopped seeing me. I didn't know until Tyler and I went to the university that he was also seeing Courtney. She apparently found out about us and she broke it off with him after he'd already broken it off with me. We guess he thought that she was going to tell me and he couldn't handle it and killed her."

"Whoa, a real psycho, huh?" Brian asks.

"I don't really think so. I just think he couldn't have his cake and eat it, too. Anyway, he followed Tyler and me to the university. He figured out that we were going there to investigate and he knew we'd find out the truth. And it really gets ugly from here."

"Now you really have my attention. What happened next?"

"I might as well tell you that Tyler and my relationship wasn't entirely professional. We'd gotten really close before we left Palmetto for the university. Jacob knew that and was very jealous."

"What'd your boss think about that?" Brian inquires.

"He wasn't a happy camper, but he'd already pretty much figured it out on his own before Tyler told him. He was afraid that our relationship would jeopardize our safety."

"And I'm assuming it did?"

"That's an understatement. Jacob slit Amanda's throat. She was Courtney's friend from the university that was giving us all the information. He kidnaped me from her apartment and held me in an equipment shed at the university."

"Weren't you petrified?"

"Out of my wits, but I knew Tyler would find me. He did, but Jacob hurt him, too."

"Wow, go on!" Brian couldn't wait to hear more.

"We'd gotten the police involved early on and they were on his trail.

Jacob ended up running from the police, took a wrong turn and hit a construction dump truck head on. It killed him instantly."

"How about you and Tyler?" Brian asks. "Of course you are fine, but what happened to him?"

"We both ended up in the hospital, but my injuries weren't life threatening. Tyler's were worse. He'd been stabbed in the back and we thought he'd have quite a long recovery period."

"What happened with your relationship? You obviously didn't stay with him if you were married to someone else."

"He didn't want me to wait on him while he was recovering and gave me my walking papers," Samantha says sadly.

"You loved him didn't you Samantha?" Brian asks.

"Yes, I did."

"Then why didn't you fight for him?"

"I did, but he wouldn't take my phone calls," Samantha says, still wondering why she's saying all of this to him.

"And you finally just gave up?" Brian asks.

"I guess you could say that."

"This didn't happen that long ago. May I ask how your husband came into the picture?"

"I've already told you this much, I might as well continue," Samantha says, sighing.

"You don't have to if you don't want to."

"My husband worked at *The Tribune* also. He was a really good friend all through my grieving process over Tyler and our relationship changed. I fell in love with him," Samantha says and tears well up in her eyes.

"I see this is very painful for you," Brian says, frowning.

"Right before our wedding Tyler found out from George we were about to get married. He finally came to his senses and came to see me. I told him I still loved him, but I wasn't in love with him anymore and he went back to Pittsburgh."

"Ouch!" Brian says. "Must have been painful for Tyler."

"I'm sure it was. But he wouldn't accept any of my phone calls, wouldn't call me and wanted no contact at all. I had to move on with my life."

"And you married, Todd, end of story," Brian says.

"Pretty much." Samantha sighs. "Then a year later and Todd's taken from me too. And guess who shows up at Todd's funeral?"

"No way!" Brian exclaims. "He didn't."

"Tyler was there. George thought it might help in some way. Instead it just brought it all back again."

"No wonder you're getting away for a while. I think you deserve it."

"I need to get my life on track again and see where I want to go from here."

"I have one question."

"What is it?" Samantha asks.

"Do you still have feelings for Tyler? I have a feeling deep down you do."

"Right now I'm not sure about anything. I really don't think I do, though."

"Only time will tell. Now, let's talk about something more pleasant, okay?"

The two of them have talked so long they can't believe they are approaching the one stop of the flight in Denver.

"Looks like we are about to land." Brian says to Samantha, looking over her out the window.

"I guess I pretty much monopolized your time, didn't I?"

"Think nothing of it. It was very interesting."

"Don't we have a small layover here?" Brian asks.

"I think we have about forty-five minutes." Samantha says, looking out her window and seeing the snow on the mountains.

"Want to go into the airport and grab a bite while we're waiting?" Brian asks Samantha.

"Sounds like a great idea. I'm tired of sitting and ready to walk."

Chapter Twelve

Brian and Samantha make small talk during the rest of the flight. They are about to land on the island of Oahu and are both staring out the window.

"The ocean sure beats the snowy mountains in Denver doesn't it?" Brian asks.

"Sure does and I can hardly wait to sit my butt on that beach," Samantha says, smiling.

Brian is thinking to himself that he'd like to see her in her bathing suit on that beach. He's been quite impressed with Samantha the whole trip out and he's wondering just how to approach seeing her again. He knows she's staying on this island but he doesn't know where and is a little apprehensive about asking her. He understands she's grieving for her husband and it's only been a few short weeks. He's sure she isn't looking for a relationship, but neither is he. He'd just like to see her again. Being in beautiful Hawaii and not having someone to share it with is lonesome. He'll just have to find a way to approach the subject.

The plane lands and the two of them gather up their belongings and are ready to depart the plane.

"Samantha, follow me and I'll take you to the baggage claim."

"Thanks, you lead and I'll follow," she says, following him off the plane.

They reach the baggage claim and their luggage has yet to arrive. It gives Brian the opportunity to find out where she's staying.

"Do you have a car rented Samantha or are you taking a taxi to your hotel?" Brian asks, putting his hands in his pockets.

"No, I'm going to grab a taxi. I thought I'd get acclimated to my surroundings for a day or so then I'll rent a car when I'm ready to sight see."

"I've got a car rented. Why don't you let me take you to your hotel?" Brian asks, hoping she says yes.

"I don't want to put you out. I'm sure you have lots to do with your convention going on. I can grab a taxi, but thanks anyway."

"Don't be silly. I don't have to check in for the convention until in the morning."

"What hotel is your convention?" Samantha asks innocently. Little does she know Brian is trying to find out where she's staying.

"The convention's at the Omni and that's where I'm registered."

"That's where I'm staying," Samantha says, a little shocked that out of all the hotels on the island they are at the same one.

"Then that settles it. You're riding with me. It'd be crazy for you to take a taxi when we're going to the same one. Unless you're uneasy about going with me, since we just met. If that's the case then I understand completely. Believe me my intentions are honorable."

"I wasn't even thinking that, but I guess I should be. Everyone says I'm too trusting at times and I guess this is one of them. After spending that many hours on the flight with you and telling you all about myself, I guess I might as well trust you enough to get me to my hotel."

Brian is ecstatic that they'll be staying at the same hotel. This means that he will be running into her from time to time and maybe he can arrange to spend some more time with her.

Their luggage finally makes it around the turnstile and both of them collect their respective bags.

Noticing the large suitcase that Samantha retrieves, Brian remarks, "Looks like you've packed for months, Samantha. How long do you plan on staying?"

Laughing she says, "I know I'm a typical female. I packed practically everything I own as far as summer clothes go and I more than likely won't wear half of them. But you know the old scout motto: *Always be prepared.*"

Brian retrieves his luggage and only has a small suitcase and suit bag. "Doesn't look like you are staying very long, Brian. How long does the convention run?"

"Just four days," he remarks. "Not nearly as long as I'd like to stay in this beautiful state. I need to go check on my rental car. You want to stay here or go with me?"

"I'll go with you if you don't mind. I'd rather be walking than sitting any longer."

The place to pick up the rental car was just up one floor and they take the escalator. Brian's rental car was ready and waiting out front. He'd told them what airlines and flight number he'd be arriving on so his car would be ready.

Walking away from the counter, he approaches Samantha. "The cars already out front and waiting, come on."

"Nice car!" Samantha exclaims as they approach the car that's parked right outside the terminal. It's a red convertible, but not knowing car models very well she doesn't know what make it is, as if it matters anyway.

"I told you this time I was going to do some sightseeing, so I rented a convertible," he says, opening the trunk. "What better way to see Hawaii." He opens the trunk and throws their luggage in. "Let's go for a ride, want to? We still have some daylight left."

"Sure, I'm on no schedule," Samantha says as Brian opens her door for her and she climbs in and they take off. They've only reached the ocean and are driving alongside it, enjoying the view when she suddenly gets this huge feeling of guilt. "Brian, I don't think I should be doing this."

"Why not?" he shouts in order for her to hear him over the wind and traffic. "Aren't you enjoying the ride?" He looks over and tears are streaming down her face. "Samantha, what's wrong?" he asks and pulls over to the side of the rode.

"It hasn't even been two months since I lost Todd and I'm taking a ride with another man. And I must say, a complete stranger. What am I doing anyway?" she asks, covering her face with her hands.

"Samantha, number one, I'm not a complete stranger and number two, we are just taking a ride. You are doing nothing wrong and I have nothing but honorable intentions where you are concerned. I have no intention of making any moves on you. I understand completely where you are coming from. I just thought I could be your friend."

"I'm so sorry, Brian," she says, resting her hand on his arm.

"If you want to go to the hotel now I'll be more than happy to take you," he says, watching for her reaction.

"Will you please? I hate it that I've ruined your ride, but I think I'd like to check in now. I promised my parents that I would let them know as soon as I got here. They will be expecting a call from me soon,"

Brian drives her to the hotel and the doorman takes her luggage and she follows him to the front desk. Separate clerks check each of them in and when they are finished they are ready to go their separate ways.

"Samantha, it's been great getting to know you and sitting beside you on the plane. I'm sorry about the ride, but maybe you'll let me take you on another one before I leave to go back to the New York."

"Likewise, Brian. Thanks so much for being a shoulder to lean on. I don't know if I'll be able to take you up on that ride, though. I have a lot of thinking to do. I need some time alone to do that."

"Then let's just say goodbye and maybe I'll run into you during my stay here," he says, extending his arm to shake her hand.

"Goodbye, Brian, and thanks again," she says, exchanging his handshake.

Chapter Thirteen

Samantha makes an early night of it once she's unpacked her things. She hasn't realized how tired she is from the long flight. Her alarm goes off the next morning and she can't believe that it's already morning. She sits up, stretches and puts her legs over the side of the bed. Rising, she walks over to the window that is covered with plantation shutters and opens them. The sun is just coming up over the water and the sight is breathtaking. The reflection on the ocean is awesome. She can hardly wait to throw on a pair of shorts and a t-shirt and take a walk on the beach. She loves doing this at home, but being in Hawaii is entirely different.

During her walk back hunger pains start attacking. She's already lost too much weight and her mother is concerned about her. She needs to eat to keep her strength up. She finds a little table in the corner at the hotel restaurant, orders juice, a bowl of fruit and a bagel. While she's waiting on her food she sees Brian in the restaurant doorway and he's spotted her.

Walking over to her, he says, "Good morning, Samantha, how are you?"

"Good morning, Brian. I'm just fine. I just took a walk on the beach as the sun came up. It was beautiful. Doesn't your convention start this morning?"

"No, that's tomorrow. Today is Sunday, remember?" he says, smiling down at her.

"Oops, I guess it is. How soon my days get mixed up when I'm out of my routine. Would you like to join me?"

"If you don't mind, I'd like that. Are you sure it's okay?" he asks, not wanting to upset her already this morning.

"Sit down. I don't like eating alone," she says and makes a motioning gesture with her hand for him to sit down.

The waitress arrives with her breakfast and asks Brian if he'd like to order. He does so and they make small talk until his breakfast arrives.

"What's on your agenda today?" she asks.

"Nothing much. I'm just going to lounge around the beach and pool and take advantage until the meetings start tomorrow. How about you, what are you planning for your first day here?" he asks, taking a drink of his water.

"I'm just going to relax, read and soak up some sun," she says, smoothing cream cheese on her bagel.

Not much is said while they are eating. He gets the impression that she's a little withdrawn this morning and that maybe he ought to leave well enough alone. He'd like to spend some more time with her, but maybe he'd better give her a little space. Under any other circumstances he'd make a move towards her, but in this case he'd better take it slow. He has no intentions of giving up, but maybe he'll have a better chance with her if he's not pushy. On the other hand, though, he only has four days on the island and time will be of the essence if he plans on spending more of it with her.

Finishing his coffee, he wipes his mouth with his white cloth napkin and sets it down next to his empty plate. "Samantha, thanks for the company. I hope you enjoy your first day here and don't get sunburned," he says, sliding his chair out and standing up.

"Leaving already?" she asks, trying to swallow the last bite of her bagel and cream cheese.

"Yeah, I think so. You take care and maybe I'll run into you again soon," he says and starts to walk away.

"Brian," she says, rising from her chair, "I'm sorry I'm not a very good conversationalist this morning."

"That's okay, you have a nice day," he says and walks away, knowing full well that he doesn't want to leave her there alone. He's getting frustrated, but doesn't know how to handle the situation. It's way too early for her to even think of another man, but damn it, there's something about her that's driving him crazy.

Samantha's finished, so she motions for the waitress. The waitress takes her ticket and credit card and says she'll return with her receipt in a minute. She's decided she'll go back to her room, change into her bathing suit and head for the pool. It's still early and the sun hasn't had a chance to heat up yet. She might have a chance to soak some up without burning too much.

Dressed in her pink two-piece suit with the hint of mint green pin stripes and a mint green cover up she decides to lie by the pool that overlooks the ocean. There are three pools at the hotel, but this is the only one that overlooks the ocean. This way, she can have the best of both worlds. She lays her beach towel over the chaise and puts her book, lotion, and sunscreen on the table provided next to the chaise. As she removes her cover-up she doesn't see Brian lounging at the other end of the pool. There are so many people already around the pool, she doesn't even notice him.

Brian does see her, however, and is watching her remove the mint green cover-up, revealing the pink two-piece suit underneath. He can't help but notice the body in the suit. "How in this world am I gonna be able to keep my distance?" he asks himself. "Leave it to me to find a beautiful girl who has just lost her husband. God help you, Brian!" He sighs as he wipes his forehead with the back of his hand. He decides not to approach her again so soon and lies on his stomach, which will still allow him a view of her, but she cannot see him.

Lying down on her stomach, she unties the strings on her bra top so she won't get tan marks on her neck and shoulders. As she does so, it reveals a little more of her, which Brian doesn't hesitate to notice.

Relaxation is exactly what the doctor ordered and she fully intends to follow his orders and this is a great start.

A sudden noise awakens Samantha. She doesn't realize that she's been asleep for over an hour. Sitting up she grabs her straps as not to expose herself as she reaches for her watch on the little white mess table beside her lounge chair and is amazed how long she's been sleeping. She ties the straps behind her neck and assesses the damage to her skin from the sun. She was sure she'd applied enough sunscreen, but notices the areas that she'd missed with the lotion. Those areas are quite red. Making a mental note to be more careful in the future, she decides she's had way too much sun and heads for her room. Not knowing that Brian is lounging by the pool and observing her every move, she has to walk past him before entering the hotel and spots him.

"Brian, I didn't know you were out here. Been out here long?" she asks, wrapping the white beach towel a little tighter around her waist.

"For a little while, I guess. I wanted to get some sun before it heated up too much. Have a nice nap, did you?" he asks, liking what he sees wrapped in the white beach towel. "You look a little pink. Are you okay?"

"I hope so. I had no intention of falling asleep, but obviously that's exactly what I did. I think I need to be a little more thorough in applying my sunscreen in the future." She rubs her shoulder that just happened to be missed with the sunscreen and was beginning to sting a little.

"It doesn't look too bad. I believe you woke up just in time."

Samantha realizes that Brian was watching her sunbathe and her cheeks are turning pink, not from the sun but from embarrassment. "Obviously, you knew I was out here. Why didn't you come over and say something?" she asks, pushing her light brown hair out of her eyes and sliding the left side behind her ear.

Patting the lounge chair with his hand, he asks, "Would you like to sit down?"

Hesitating, she does so and as she sits down she takes the towel from around her waste and rests it in her lap. "I could get used to this lifestyle."

"It wouldn't take long, would it?" he says, looking out towards the ocean. "Would you like to have dinner with me this evening, Samantha?"

"I don't think I should, Brian," she says, thinking of Todd.

"You have to eat, don't you?"

"That's not the point and you know it," she says, turning to look at him.

"This may be the last time I see you with the convention starting in the morning," he says, trying to get a little bit of sympathy from her. He wouldn't be able to stand it if he couldn't see her again. If he's being too pushy, then so be it. He has to try.

"I'll tell you what, I won't have dinner with you this evening, but call me tomorrow and I'll see. I'm not making any promises, though," she says and, taking the towel off her lap, she stands up and wraps it back around her waist.

"I guess that's better than nothing," he says, standing up beside her, trying to keep his eyes focused above her neck. "May I have your room number to get in touch with you?"

"Ask the desk clerk to ring my room for you," she says, being cautious, not wanting to reveal her phone number nor her room number. Of course, all he needs to do is follow her, but she doesn't think that he would do that. She honestly thinks he meant it when he told her he wouldn't harm her. At least she hopes so.

"Fair enough," he says, realizing that she is being cautious, as she should be.

"Then I'll talk with you tomorrow. Enjoy the rest of your day," she says and starts walking for the door, fumbling for her room key.

Brian sits back down on his lounge chair and picks up the book he brought out to read. He's feeling pretty confident that when he calls her tomorrow she'll say yes.

Samantha showers and applies aloe to the areas that received a little too much sun. They turned even pinker after her shower. She'll be lucky if she's able to lie out in the sun tomorrow.

She hadn't called her parents upon her arrival. She decides to call them, so they won't worry. Calculating the time difference between here and South Carolina, she finds her cell phone and dials their number.

"Hello," her mother says.

"Hi, Mom," Samantha says, glad to hear her voice.

"Samantha, is that you?" her mother asks, not being able to hear her very well.

"Yes, Mom, it's me."

"How are you? How was your flight?"

"Fine, how's Dad?" she inquires

"He's fine, he's sitting right here. How's Hawaii?"

"Beautiful and breathtaking. Just like the pictures."

"What have you been doing? Are you getting any rest?" her mother asks, concerned.

"I just got in yesterday evening, but I did get some sun this morning. A little more than I should have, though."

"You mean you're sunburned already, Samantha?"

"A little, but not much. Brian says it isn't too bad," Samantha says, letting his name slip without evening knowing it.

"Brian?" her mother asks. "Who's Brian?"

Oops, Samantha says to herself. "No one, Mother. Just someone I met on the flight over."

"You met someone on the plane? Oh, Samantha, be careful. Is he staying in Oahu, also?"

She's wishing she hadn't let it slip. "Yes, he's staying in this hotel, too. Mother, we just met. He's very nice and he's just trying to be a friend."

"What's he doing in Hawaii?"

"Mother, it's no big deal. He's in media sales and their yearly convention is being held here."

"Where's he from?" her mother asks, wanting to know more, as she's becoming deeply concerned for her daughter's safety.

"He lives in New York City, but he flew from Palmetto. He was visiting his parents, who live in Palmetto. It was a long flight here and we just kept each other company.

"Your father wants to speak with you," her mother says and she hands the phone to him. He's heard what her mother has said and he's concerned, also.

"Hi, honey, how're you doing?"

"Hi, Dad. I'm okay," she says, waiting for him to preach to her, also.

"You have to be careful, sweetheart. It's hard telling what this guy has in mind."

"Dad, please don't you start, too. I'm fine. Brian seems to be a very nice guy and gentleman. He understands what I've been through and he's only being a friend. I don't want you or Mother to worry."

"We both want you to have a nice time and try to put what's happened behind you. Just please be careful! Here's your mother back. I love you." He then hands the receiver back to her.

"Mother, I have to go now. My reception is fading. I'll call in a few days."

"Please be careful, Samantha. I love you, bye."

"Love you, too, bye." She hangs up the phone and sits down on the bed, sighing. She knows what the discussion around the table will be now.

"Did she even mention Todd to you on the phone?" her mother asks, turning and asking her father.

"No, why?" her father asks. "We only discussed this guy she met. You heard me tell her we are concerned and for her to be careful."

"Why wouldn't she mention Todd? For crying out loud, she just buried him!"

"I don't know, but she didn't. Now don't get all bent out of shape. She said he's just someone she met on the long flight to Hawaii and he's just being a friend and we have to trust she knows what she's doing. We have to give her time to grieve in her own way. She'll be fine."

"But that doesn't mean I won't worry just the same," she says, putting her hands on her hips.

"She'll call again in a few days and we'll see what she has to say. But in the mean time, we have to trust her."

Chapter Fourteen

Samantha's mother runs into George at the local diner the day after talking with Samantha and is shocked to say the least that Tyler is with him.

"Hello, George," she says, approaching their table.

"Hello, Marty," George says, rising to greet her and kissing her on the cheek. "First time I've seen you since Todd's funeral. How's the family doing? Have you heard from Samantha?"

Not answering George, she remarks to Tyler, "And Tyler, I'm surprised to see you still here. I thought you went back to Pittsburgh after our son-in-law's funeral."

"Hello, Mrs. Summers, nice to see you again. I haven't been able to return to Pittsburgh yet. And I must say, I'm enjoying the weather down here a lot more than what is in Pittsburgh at the moment."

"Won't you have a seat, Marty?" George asks her. "Care to join us for lunch?"

"No, thank you, George, I'm meeting a friend of mine," she says, glad that she does have an excuse. George is such a good friend, but she wouldn't join him with Tyler present even if she weren't meeting her girlfriend for lunch. He's not one of her favorite people and she definitely doesn't care to have lunch with him. "But maybe some other time."

"Sure, I'll hold you to that."

"Tyler, why are you still here in Palmetto?" Marty asks, wishing he'd be as far away from here as he could.

Looking at George, wondering if he should tell her the truth, he decides what the hell. Besides, what's he got to lose? Maybe she'll just let it slip to Samantha that he's filing in for her. "I've been filling in for your daughter at the paper since Todd's tragic accident."

"You what!" Marty exclaims, surprised. "Samantha never mentioned it to me."

"That's because she doesn't know," George pipes in. "I thought it better she didn't. As far as she knows, Lee's filling in for her and I'd like to keep it that way. Tyler is much more qualified for her position than Lee and we both felt Tyler was the best one right now."

"I don't think that she'll be thrilled to hear this, George."

"I'd rather you didn't mention it to her, either. Worrying about her job here and who's doing it for her is the last thing she needs on her mind right now. And she certainly doesn't need to know it's Tyler."

"Mrs. Summers, I think you know how I feel about your daughter. I'd do anything for her. When George called me and told me what had happened I knew I wanted to do this for her. It's the least I can do after what I put her through. And if I could go back and undo the damage I've done, I'd do it in a heartbeat. I only hope that one day I'll get the chance."

"I hope not in this lifetime," Marty says, sneering at him."

"Have you heard anything from Samantha?" George asks again, quickly trying to end the current trend of the conversation.

Not wanting to acknowledge his question the second time, but not wanting to seem rude either, she decides to answer. "Yes, she checked in yesterday."

"Is she enjoying the rest and relaxation?" George asks.

"She'd only been there a day, but she seemed to be having a good time. She mentioned this guy who sat next to her on the long flight to Hawaii and he just happens to be staying in the same hotel. I must admit her father and I are more than a little concerned."

"And why is that?" Tyler asks, becoming very inquisitive.

"She couldn't quit talking about him and, the thing is, she never even mentioned Todd. It's only been a few weeks since the funeral and it just isn't Samantha not to even mention him."

"Wow, that is odd," George says, concerned. "That doesn't sound like Samantha at all. She was so in love with Todd and devastated the last time I spoke to her. Maybe she's just hung up in the whole trip and wanting to put it all behind her. It's going to take her a long time to get over him. Maybe this guy is just being a friend and that may be what she needs right now. She has to mourn in her own way. I wouldn't worry too much. She has a level head on her shoulders."

"We only hope she doesn't do something stupid like get involved with this guy because she's lonely. She can't even know anything about him. She hasn't had time."

Tyler's just about to go out of his mind, but he can't show his emotions. George refused to tell him where she's staying and he doesn't think Samantha's mother is aware that he doesn't know. He's hoping she'll let it slip.

"I see my girlfriend has arrived. I need to go. Nice to have run into you, George." She nods to Tyler, not saying a word.

"Hang in there, Marty," George says, standing to acknowledge her leaving. "I'm sure Samantha will be just fine."

"Thanks," Marty says and walks over to meet her friend.

"George, you are going to tell me right now where Samantha is staying," Tyler says, thumping his finger on the table.

"No, I'm not, Tyler. I told you before, I wouldn't give you any information without Samantha's permission and I meant it. I can't believe Marty let it slip and you now know she's in Hawaii."

"George, I've got to know where she's staying. What do I have to do to get it out of you? I'm going to Hawaii and find her myself if I have to. I won't be able to stand it if she's over there with some other man."

Just relax, Tyler; she's only been gone a few days. So she's met this guy. Geez, why don't you just give her the benefit of the doubt? Why does everyone immediately think something is going on? I've known Samantha since she was born and she's not about to go off and do something that stupid!" George says, pounding his fist on the table, forgetting he's in the middle of the restaurant.

"Sorry, George, I didn't mean to upset you, but you know how I feel about her."

"Yeah, and I also know the state she was in when she returned after your investigation and you gave her her walking papers. Have you forgotten that? I'll never forget the devastated look on her face and you put it there."

"Yes, and you also know I've admitted my mistake to her and to you. I know you also agree that we should still be together and that's what you want, too. You just won't admit it," Tyler says, and takes a sip of his coffee. "So how long are you going to make me wait before you tell me where she's staying, or do I have to go over there and find her myself? You know I'll do it, George!" Tyler says insistently.

"You can't go, you're covering for her here and I can't let you go."

"Lee can fill in for me, George, and we both know it! Now are you going to tell me where she's staying or am I going to find her on my own?" he asks, standing up and throwing his napkin down on the table.

"You're serious aren't you, Tyler? You'd go right now, wouldn't you?" George asks, watching Tyler rise.

"You damn right I will and, not only that, I am, so you might as well tell me or I'm walking out of here!"

"Calm down, Tyler. Give me time to think about it and we'll talk some more when we get back to the office," he says, taking a drink.

"There's no thinking about it, George!" Tyler says, sitting back down. "I'll finish lunch, but when we get back you're going to tell me. With or without your help, I'm going to Hawaii!" he says and picks up the half of his sandwich he hasn't eaten.

"Why don't you wait until she gets back? Give her the space and time she deserves and maybe your chances will be greater when she returns. When she finds out that you covered for her while she was gone, she'll be very grateful. That should give you a feather in your cap."

"Are you kidding me? And give this creep time to move on her! Not on your life!

George and Tyler finish their lunch in silence and walk back to the office. Upon returning, George walks into his office and Tyler walks a few steps further to Samantha's office, neither of them exchanging a word. Once in Samantha's office, Tyler sits at her desk and is unable to get his mind back on business and off of Samantha being in Hawaii with a guy she's just met and doesn't know a thing about. He's becoming very paranoid, worried and wondering what this guy's intentions are. Picking up the phone he dials the airlines for available flights, but before anyone can answer he hangs up. He realizes he can't do a thing until George tells him which island she's on and the hotel, so he pushes himself away from her desk and heads for his office.

"George," Tyler says, standing in the doorway. "Are you going to tell me or not?"

"Sit down, Tyler. Yes, I'll tell you, but you have to make me a promise before I tell you anything!" he says, motioning for Tyler to take a seat.

"Anything, George, I'll promise you anything. What it is?" he asks, sitting in the chair, resting his elbows on his knees, giving George his undivided attention.

Looking at him, George sees the love he has for Samantha and he really doesn't know why he's keeping her whereabouts from him. But he can't bear to see her hurting again. "If I give it to you, you have to promise not to hurt her again. I don't know what she'll do when she sees you, but I know she'll blame me if anything goes wrong. She'll know I was the one that told you where she's staying because she knows her parents would never tell you."

"A little time is all I need, George. I know deep down she still loves me. She as much told me so before she married Todd."

"I believe you told me she said she still loved you, but wasn't *in* love with you anymore," George says, pushing his chair away from his desk a little to open the middle drawer to pull something out.

"I really think I can win her love again. I have to at least try. What we had was special and you know that. If it wasn't for my injury we'd more than likely be married by now, wouldn't we?"

"Yeah, yeah, yeah," he says and throws the piece of paper he pulls from his desk across at him.

Tyler picks up the paper to see what is on it and a smile starts to form across his face. "Thanks, George. You don't know what this means to me."

"I think I do, Tyler. Just don't blow it this time. You'd better have a talk with Lee to see if he will cover for you while you're gone. How soon are you planning to leave?"

"As soon as I can convince Lee to cover for me and book a flight."

"Then get the hell out of here. But remember, Tyler, she gave you a chance and you turned her away. Just be prepared for the rejection if she says no. She's a very vulnerable young lady right now and you'll have to treat her with kid gloves."

"Thanks, George, I owe you for this one!" he says and heads to find Lee.

Lee agrees to take over Samantha's office during Tyler's absence, but isn't pleased. He's been super busy the past few weeks, working on a new case that George assigned him, but he knows come hell or high water Tyler's going to Hawaii to find Samantha. Once Tyler's told him what she's up to in Hawaii Lee pretty much agrees with him that someone should be checking up on her, and knowing how Tyler feels about her he'd do the same thing if the tables were turned.

"I'll make it up to you, I promise," Tyler tells Lee.

"Your damn right you will, buddy," Lee says, pointing a finger at Tyler. "And believe me I'll get my payback when you return. Now get on out of here. Give my best to Samantha when you find her. That is if she even speaks to you."

"I will and thanks again. I won't forget what you've done for me!" Tyler says, extending his arm to shake Lee's hand.

It takes Tyler a few days to get everything in order, filling Lee in on what he's been working on for Samantha, and still manages to find a flight out on Friday morning to Oahu.

Chapter Fifteen

"Samantha. Great seeing you again," Brian says, running into her at the elevator. "I've been busy with the convention the last few days. Are you enjoying your stay?" he asks, shuffling the papers he's accumulated from the day's meetings. "Sorry I didn't get back with you after our last meeting to take you to dinner. I thought you needed some time alone, so I haven't bothered you. I hope you're not upset."

"Hi, Brian, nice to see you, too. I wondered why you didn't call, but I understand," she says, embarrassed, not expecting to run into him. She's in her bathing suit and carrying her cover-up from her afternoon at the beach.

"Looks like you've soaked up some sun," he says, rubbing his finger over her cheek. "You've gotten a little pink again today."

Samantha gets a few goose bumps down her arm as he rubs his finger over her cheek, assessing what damage the sun has done to her face. Bringing her hand to her face, she replies, "Am I red?"

"Just a little, but not much, it adds a little more color to your face."

The elevator stops at the bottom floor and the doors open. "After you," Brian says.

"Thanks," Samantha says and, as she steps into the elevator, she notices no one else is there to enter. She feels a little self-conscious, stepping in and it only being the two of them.

"What floor are you on?" he asks after pushing button number six for his floor.

"I'm on six, also," she replies, not believing that they haven't run into each other sooner.

"Wow. I didn't know we're on the same floor. It's a wonder we haven't run into each other before now."

"I've been sleeping in and you've probably been up and going early," she replies, tightening the towel around her waist. She sure wishes she'd taken time to put on her cover-up before leaving the beach.

"I have been up fairly early for the meetings, but today was our last day of long meetings. Do you have any plans for tomorrow?"

"No, my social calendar is wide open."

"How about taking another ride with me? We can take a picnic lunch and see where we end up."

"Okay, sounds great. As long as…" She hesitates.

"As long as what?" Brian asks.

"As long as you're not expecting too much from me."

"I know, I know. Samantha, how many times does a guy have to say it? It's only a picnic. Will you come?"

"Sure, and I'm sorry. It's just that I don't want you to get your hopes up. I'm not looking for a relationship right now."

"Who said anything about a relationship? This is a picnic." He's wondering what it's going to take to break down that barrier. "I'll pick you up at nine am sharp," he replies as the elevator hits the sixth floor. "After you, madam," he says, motioning for her to get off the elevator first.

"I can be ready by then. Do I need to bring anything?" she asks, fumbling for her key card. Her room is down about four doors on the right.

"Nope, I'll take care of everything. I mean I'll have the hotel take care of everything." He's laughing as he corrects himself. He notices that she's stopped and reached her room. His is only two doors down on the left and he likes the idea that his is this close to hers and wishes he'd known sooner. He would have had a bottle of wine sent up and called her for a nightcap.

"Where's your room?" she asks, realizing it can't be far from hers because he hasn't stopped yet.

"Two doors down on the left. It's beyond me why we haven't run into each other on occasion."

"Me, too," Samantha replies. "Well, I'll see you in the morning then."

"See you," Brian says and walks towards his room, knowing full well he'd rather be going to hers.

Brian knocks on her door at nine a.m. sharp in a pair of navy blue shorts, yellow t-shirt, wearing sneakers and holding a picnic basket.

Samantha's just coming out of the bathroom after her final inspection when she hears the knock. She's wearing white shorts, red t-shirt and has a red and white polka dotted scarf around her neck. She brushes her hands down the front of her shorts as sort of a last minute fix as she answers the knock. Before she opens the door she looks out the hole in the door to see if it indeed is Brian and she sees the picnic basket. Laughing, she opens the door.

"What are you laughing at, Samantha? Never seen a guy holding a picnic basket before?" he asks, noticing how tough she looks in her outfit.

"I'm sorry, it just struck me funny. Come in," she says, pulling the door open, allowing him entrance.

"Are you ready to go?"

"Sure am, just let me grab my purse. How'd the hotel do filling that basket for you?"

"I'm impressed. They put in just what I'd suggested, plus a little more."

"Where are we going?" Samantha asks, putting her purse strap over her shoulder.

"Not far. If you're ready let's go." He opens the door for her, follows her out and the door locks automatically behind them.

In the hotel parking garage Brian puts the picnic basket in the small trunk of the Mazda, walks around to open the door for Samantha then gets behind the wheel.

"I thought we'd go to the beach, take a walk, get to know each other a little more, eat, then take that afternoon ride I promised you. How's that sound to you?" he asks, starting the car and putting it in reverse.

"Great. I love this little car and I'm so looking forward to the ride."

The ride down the beach is beautiful. The waves today are higher than normal and are crashing up on the beach. With the top down the air is blowing Samantha's hair all over her face and she's trying to put it back in place but knows it's a lost cause. She decides to just let it fly and enjoy the ride. She can fix it later. Brian notices she's concerned about it and reaches over to put the left side behind her ear knowing full well it won't stay, but at least he gets an innocent opportunity to touch her face again. He thinks she's so pretty and is anxious to touch more than just there. He knows it's going to be tough breaking down that barrier. "Samantha, would you quit fussing with your hair? It looks great blowing in the wind," he remarks as the strand he put behind her ear is again blowing in her face.

"It's a lost cause, isn't it?" she says, turning to look at him as her hair once again covers her face.

"I see a place up ahead where we can pull over. Are you ready for a walk on the beach?" he asks loudly because the wind is muffling his voice.

"I'm ready if you are." She smiles.

Brian parks the Mazda, walks around to help Samantha out and takes her hand in the process. After helping her out and shutting her door he doesn't release her hand and he's hoping that she doesn't let go. Hand in hand they head across the narrow road that runs parallel to the ocean.

"Which way do you want to walk, Samantha? To the left it seems to be less populated but there seems to be more beach homes. To the right it looks a little more touristy with restaurants and t-shirt shops. You pick."

"To the left. I love to look at the homes on the beach and pick out which one I can dream of owning. Then if you don't mind I'd like to walk the other way and pick up souvenirs for my parents."

"Then the left it is." The two of them take off on their walk.

"Do you ever dream of living in a home like this?" Samantha asks, admiring a huge three-story beach home painted a sand color with white plantation shutters on every window and a white metal roof.

"No, not really, I haven't even thought about it. In fact, isn't that mostly a girl fantasy rather than a guy thing?"

"Are you making fun of me?" she asks, still holding his hand. She pulls it away immediately, not realizing that he's been holding it all along. It feels so comfortable it feels like Todd's. Her face is turning red from embarrassment and Brian is looking down at her.

"Samantha, I'm sorry. Are you okay? It felt so comfortable and I thought you were enjoying it," he remarks, looking down at her.

"I don't know what to say. I guess I didn't pay any attention after you helped me out of the car. I'm sorry, I don't want to mislead you."

"Samantha, it's okay. You don't have to apologize," he says as he turns her towards him and looks down at her. He hovers about six inches above her and he wants her to look at him, so he pulls her chin up to meet his eyes. "Please don't be embarrassed. I think you know by now, even though we've only been together such a short time, that there is something between us."

"No, you're wrong. I can't feel anything for you. I just lost my husband such a short time ago." The tears are starting to sting her eyes.

"I know what you're saying, Samantha, but you know you feel it and so do I. Now admit it. You can't go back and you definitely can't bring Todd back. It was very unfortunate, but you have to go on with your life."

"So soon?" she asks, the tears now running down her cheeks. "This is so unfair to him."

"Think about it, Samantha. Would he have wanted you to suffer? Granted, it's a little soon, okay maybe a lot too soon, but we can't help what we feel." In saying this he tries to pull her closer to him and she balks.

"Please, Brian," she says, pushing him away. "I don't have any feelings for you. I need to go back. Will you take me now?" She's become aware that this whole idea is scaring her. She doesn't know whether she's having second thoughts or is afraid of her true feelings. She can't decipher now, but she knows she needs to get away from him and she turns to head back to the car.

Brian grabs her elbow as she turns to leave. "Samantha, don't go."

Knowing full well she should keep on walking without turning around, she doesn't heed her own advice. Instead she stops to look up at him when he grabs her elbow and sees a look in his eyes she knows she should leave well enough alone.

"I mean it, Samantha. Please don't make me take you back," he begs, still holding onto her elbow with all he's got.

That's all it takes. That look, those words and all that she's been through, she can't take any more, she all but falls into his arms. "I don't know what the hell I'm doing, but please just hold me."

In an instant, Brian has her in his arms and is holding her as tight as he can without squeezing the life out of her, in hopes that this is the beginning of something wonderful. He combs a few strands of her hair out of her face with his fingers as she sobs in his hold.

"Do you want to go back?" he asks, holding on to her and praying she'll say no.

She's having a hard time getting her emotions under control and stays as close to his chest as she possibly can. She doesn't want to let go as the weeks of sorrow pour out. She doesn't know if she's holding on for her feelings towards him or not wanting to let go for fear of falling deeper into sadness. "Please just hold me a while longer."

Brian holds on to her for what seems to be an eternity. Thankfully, this end of the beach isn't as populated. Only the people who own the beach homes are here and aren't interested in what is going on with anyone but themselves. Most all of the other vacationers are on the other end by the restaurants and souvenir shops.

Her sobs subside and she releases the tight hold she has on him and he loosens his arms around her. "Going to be okay?" he asks, rubbing his hand down her back. He doesn't want to let her go and he'd really like to try and kiss her but he doesn't want to take advantage when her defenses are down.

"I think so. I'm so sorry for falling apart on you," she says, looking up at him while wiping the tears from her face.

Looking down and seeing the sadness in her eyes he can't stand it any longer. He bends his head down and plants a soft kiss on her lips. Fortunately for him she doesn't pull away. She responds back.

The kiss sends tingles down her whole body and she can't believe she's letting him kiss her and what's more she can't believe she's kissing him back. The kiss seems to melt the weeks of sadness. Right now she just feels the longing as she moves back into his arms. The kiss gets deeper and she doesn't want to pull away.

Brian takes her back into his arms and holds her tight while kissing her again. He knows full well this isn't right but he can't help himself and doesn't want to. Neither of them seems to care the people on the beach are now watching them.

"Samantha, what are we going to do?" he whispers, pulling away from the kiss. "I've only got the rest of today and tomorrow and I'll be flying back to New York. I have to be back to work on Monday."

"I'm planning to stay a couple more weeks as planned. I don't want to go back too soon. I need this time away."

"I only have a few vacation days left. I was planning to take them over Easter. We'll just have to make the best of today and tomorrow." He kisses her again and this time he's moving his hands over her lower back pulling her in close to him not leaving any room in between.

The closeness of Brian feels so comforting to Samantha. She becomes very submissive to his hold, knowing full well what this could mean. Fortunately, for her they are on the beach and there's not a lot he can do about it right now, not that she doesn't want it also.

After what seems like an eternity he releases his hold and she looks up at him and smiles. The look she gives him makes him want her even more.

"You're beautiful, Samantha," he says, wanting to take her right here and now.

"What are we going to do?"

"Let's just enjoy the rest of today and tomorrow and then we'll figure out things from there. Are you hungry?" He's just trying to forget about what he really wants right now and what they need to do with the situation as it is.

"Yes, I'm hungry. Let's get the picnic basket. I'm anxious to see what the hotel's fixed you up with."

They walk the short distance back to the car hand in hand to retrieve the basket. Samantha carries the blanket and they find a place on the beach to enjoy their lunch.

"Wow, they did a great job packing this!" she says, pulling the fried chicken, assortment of veggies, cheeses, fruits, breads, and a bottle of white wine from the packed basket.

They both enjoy the tasty lunch and are munching on the fruit as she's resting comfortably against him on the blanket watching the foam from the salt-water landing on the beach and making it's way back out. It seemed neither of them needed to say a word. Everything just feels right.

"Are you ready for that ride I promised you?"

Looking up at him and taking another bite out of her apple, she mumbles yes. Getting up on her knees, she starts putting the remains of their lunch back into the basket. "That was a great lunch. They did a good job. Why does it always taste better when you don't have to fix it yourself?"

"I wouldn't know that answer, I never cook." He smiles and helps her clean up the mess.

Brian picks up the basket as Samantha shakes the sand out of the blanket, folds it and they head back to the car.

Once at the car they put the basket and blanket back in the tiny trunk and Brian follows Samantha to her side and opens the door. But before she can get in he stops her, leans against the car and pulls her into him and kisses her. This time she puts her arms around his neck and kisses him back.

"I think this will be a short ride," he says, looking down at her with his arms still around her resting on her waist.

Samantha has this little voice going off in the back of her mind telling her to stop this before it's too late, but she's not listening. Too many negative things have happened to her when she falls in love so she's going to throw caution to the wind. First, it was Jacob dropping her like a hot potato when he was having the affair with Courtney at the same time. Then there was Tyler when he was stabbed by Jacob and couldn't see her taking care of him if he'd been an invalid. She thought she'd seen the end to her sadness when she married Todd then he was suddenly taken from her also. Life's too short and she isn't going to let Brian get away. God must have sent him her way for a reason and she's going to live for the moment because tomorrow may never come.

"Then a short ride it is," she says, planting a light kiss on him, then gets in on her side of the car. "Let's go."

Of course, Brian isn't going to take any time. He practically runs around the car, jumps in and turns the key in the ignition.

Chapter Sixteen

Tyler's flight arrives on time. The flight's been very long with only a couple stops along the way and he's definitely exhausted. He was only able to take a couple short naps because he'd had Samantha on his mind.

He makes his way to the baggage claim to retrieve his luggage, then decides he'd better check on his car rental. He doesn't know how long he'll be here but he wants to have a car at his disposal if he expects to watch Samantha's comings and goings.

Everything runs smoothly at the car rental counter and he's told his car will be waiting out front of the terminal under their rental sign. A few minutes later he throws his luggage in the trunk and he's ready to find the Omni. Of course it wasn't easy getting the name of the hotel out of George, but he'd succeeded and nothing was going to stop him from finding her now.

The doorman greets Tyler when he arrives at the Omni and once inside he notices the check-in counter is extremely busy. Looking at his watch he notices it's almost six and the normal time for a lot of arrivals.

He'd seen the entry to one of the hotel bars on his right when he came in and decides to have a drink and wait till the check-in line thins out. Upon entering the bar he catches a glimpse out of his right eye of a couple coming through the front door and glancing in that direction he sees Samantha with a man at her side. Thinking to himself this must be the guy Samantha's mother was telling George about. Fortunately for him she doesn't see him. He steps to his right and stands close to the doorway at the entrance to the bar. He's out of her sight but he can still see her. Observing them approach the elevator they seem awfully friendly for having just met. In fact he's holding her hand and this irritates him.

Tyler's had several hours on the flight over to decide what he's going to say to her when the time comes. He's definitely sure the time *will* come. He hasn't flown thousands of miles to go back home empty handed. His hopes are to have her by his side when he makes the flight back to Palmetto. But he doesn't want to approach her right now. He wants to wait a day or two to see just how close she's gotten to this guy.

They are the only two waiting to get on the next available elevator and as the door closes he hurries over to see what floor the elevator stops on. He will at least know what floor to watch.

After a couple drinks Tyler notices the line at the check-in counter is much shorter. He pays his tab, leaves a tip for the bartender and meanders over to check in. At the counter he answers all the normal questions asked during check-in then the clerk hands him his room key and proceeds to tell him what floor he's on and how to get there.

Reaching the elevator he starts to push the right number on the number pad and realizes it's the same floor Samantha and her man friend were getting off on. What a coincidence he says to himself. It's going to be easier than he thought watching her. That is if they are on the same floor. He did notice they pushed one button but that doesn't necessarily mean they are on the same floor. They could have been going to either his or her room.

No one is in the hallway when Tyler approaches his room. Upon entering he finds his room to be of great satisfaction. Working for the paper in Pittsburgh he'd been in some fancy hotels but none of this caliber. He could get use to this luxury. His luggage is already in the room and put away, what an amenity. Walking over and opening the sliding glass door he can hear the ocean below and looking to his right he can see a huge part of the city. He knows he's going to enjoy his stay here. That is, if he can talk some sense into Samantha. Little does he know what is taking place in her room across the hall from him right at this minute.

Once in her room Samantha and Brian are throwing caution to the wind. They hardly hear the door close behind them before they are all over each other.

"Samantha?" Brian asks, breathing heavy. "Are you sure this is what you want?"

"Yes," she says, looking up at him with her arms locked around his neck.

Picking her up, he lays her on the king size bed then goes over and opens the sliding glass door. Hearing the ocean below and feeling the breeze coming in adds just what he wants to the atmosphere. Walking back to the bed, he's pulling his shirt out of his pants and lies down beside her, laying his arm over her waist and pulling her towards him.

Samantha responds to his pulling her towards him and leaves no room between the two of them when she wriggles even closer.

There is nothing left of either of them once they've made love, not once, but twice, and they drift off to sleep in each other's arms.

Samantha awakens to find Brian sitting out on their balcony in only his boxers with his feet propped up on the wrought iron railing. Grabbing the sheet off the bed to wrap her naked body in, she joins him and, as she does, she notices he's staring off into space with a puzzled look on his face.

"Are you alright?" she asks. "Did I do anything wrong?"

"No, why?" he asks, pulling her down on his lap. "Mm, you look nice in that sheet. Can I see what's under there?" He reaches for her bare skin under the sheet, laying his hand on her stomach.

"Brian! Someone may be watching us," she says as he gives her goose bumps while moving his thumb over her mid-section.

"All the way up here? I don't think so." He doesn't stop.

"Are you hungry?" he asks.

"A little."

"Want to go out for dinner or get room service?" he asks, hoping she says room service. He'd just as soon stay right here with her in what she has on right now.

"Room service is fine," she says, smiling. "I need to take a shower though."

"You take a shower and I'll order dinner. I need to check my messages in my room anyway and I can take a shower there. By that time dinner should be here. And Samantha, make sure when I return you're wearing what you have on now."

Samantha looked down and then back up at him smiling.

Brian goes down the hall to his room and upon entering sees the red light flashing on his phone. He needs to listen to the messages but knows whom they are likely from and he chooses to take a shower instead. Right now nothing is going to ruin this night. He dials room service to order their dinner and realizes he hadn't even asked Samantha what she'd like so he takes a stab at it and orders both filet and lobster, baked potato, bread, and strawberries for dessert.

Back in Samantha's room she showers, fixes her hair and sprays a little cologne over her naked body. There isn't any choice in what she's going to wear. Smiling, she takes off the bathrobe the hotel provided and grabs the sheet she threw on the bed before taking her shower. She feels a little embarrassed wearing it now that the heat of the moment is gone, but puts it on anyway.

It isn't a half hour before Brian's knocking on her door. At least she hopes this is who it is. She wouldn't want anyone else being on the other side of that door with her dressed or rather undressed as she is.

Looking through the peephole she sees him standing on the other side and she can't believe what he's wearing.

"Will you get in here?" she says, grabbing his arm and pulling him in. He's wearing paisley silk boxer shorts and a matching short silk robe. Looking up and down the hall before closing the door she sees no one.

"I thought maybe you'd feel a little uncomfortable if I came back dressed in street clothes, so I wore this," he says and pirouettes for her.

"You're nuts!" She laughs, holding tighter to her sheet because it feels like it's slipping.

Grabbing her, he kisses her and the cold bottle of wine rests on her naked back. "That's cold!" she shouts. The sheet falls down to her waist.

"Hm, now that's nice," he says, taking in the scenery in front of him.

Samantha immediately pulls the sheet back up around her peeked breasts and tightens it. "You are no good!" She says as she pokes him in the chest with her finger. "I'm hungry what time is room service?" She'd like to change the subject before something gets started that neither one of them knows will stop until they're spent again.

Looking at his watch, he says, "Should be here any minute."

At that precise moment they hear a knock on the door. Looking at each other wondering who's going to answer Samantha shakes her head no. "I'm not answering that door in this!"

"Chicken." He opens the door to see the waiter with the cart full of food. "Come on in. Put it over there," he says and points to the corner by the sliding glass door.

Brian didn't bring his wallet therefore couldn't tip the waiter. "Samantha?"

She realizes what he's after and retrieves her purse to tip him and doesn't see the waiter give Brian the high sign in approval of what's she's wearing. House rules would have him fired for even making that gesture, but Brian wouldn't turn him in. He just agrees with him and gives him the high sign back.

The waiter accepts the tip, smiles and is ready to leave the room. "If there's anything I can do for you just call." And he's gone in a flash.

The meal was fantastic and they managed to finish the whole bottle of wine. The only things left are the strawberries and whipped cream because Brian wanted to eat them last. They were both a little tipsy as they moved out to the balcony to watch the sunset. Brian brought the bowl of strawberries and whipped cream out with him. Samantha starts to sit in the other chair when he pulls her down on his lap. Smiling down at him he dips a strawberry in the whipped cream and feeds it to her. She knows how sensuous this is and what will happen if they continue.

Tyler's sitting out on his balcony wondering what the two of them are doing right now when he hears a knock, which he thinks, is at his door. Walking to the door he peers through the hole and doesn't see anyone. He opens the door just as Samantha is pulling Brian into her room, but not before he sees what he's wearing and worse yet what she's not wearing. The knock he apparently heard was to her room not his. He closes the door quickly as not to be seen by her, but peers again through the hole and sees her looking up and down the hall. What she doesn't see is him watching her through his door. "Damn it Samantha!" he says out loud. "What in the hell are you doing?" He watches as she closes the door then he walks back across his room to the balcony but not before pounding the wall with his fist and retrieving a beer from the stocked refrigerator.

He is so discussed that he needs to talk to someone and decides to call George. Looking at his watch he tries to decipher the time difference and says to hell with it and calls him anyway. He doesn't care what time it is.

"Hello," George says answering the phone.

"George, it's Tyler. Were you in bed?"

"Yes, what's up?" he asks, yawning. "Do you have any idea what time it is?"

"George, I'm sorry. But I'm so upset I didn't care. I had to call," he says, taking a drink of his beer.

"Has something happened to Samantha?"

"No, not yet. But if she keeps this up it will be."

"What the hell you talking about son?" George is more than a little concerned now.

"I checked in this evening and my room just happens to be right across the hall from hers."

"How ironic. How can that make you this upset?" he asks, scratching the side of his face.

"She's not in the room by herself!"

"Are you saying she's sleeping with that guy already? Hell, she just met him. She hasn't been gone a week yet has she?" he asks, trying to make the calculations in his head.

"Just a little over a week George. I just witnessed him going into her room."

"Big deal, that doesn't mean anything does it? Are you letting your imagination run away with you?"

"It means something when all he's wearing are silk boxer shorts and a short matching robe. Oh, and by the way he was carrying a bottle of wine."

"What was Samantha wearing? Damn it Tyler, I can't believe I just asked you that."

"George, all she had on is the sheet from the bed." His voice seemed exasperated as he said it.

"Are you sure?"

"I know what I saw George! That is all she had on."

"You know you are going to have to tread lightly don't you? If she finds out you are there you might just trigger her into doing something really stupid."

"What do you call what's she doing right now? She's obviously jumping into bed with a guy she hardly knows and she just buried her husband a few weeks ago."

"I have no idea what she thinks she's doing and you've already given me more information than I need. But I agree that she's not making smart decisions. But Tyler it's her life."

"That's the hard part. I know it is, but she's obviously thinking with her heart right now and not her brain. She's devastated and looking for someone to care. I want to be that guy!"

"I hate to remind you again Tyler, but part of this is your fault and you know it."

"Yeah, yeah, yeah. Why don't you just kick me while I'm down?"

"What do you want me to do? I'm thousands of miles away."

"Nothing. I was just so upset with what I saw that I had to talk to someone."

"What do you plan on doing now?"

"I'd like to go over there right now, bust down the door, hit him in the mouth and bring Samantha over here."

"Now that would be stupid wouldn't it? I'm sure that will get you back in Samantha's good graces in a heartbeat!"

"George, I've got to take my chances. I need to let her know I'm here and why. Then if she still thinks she wants this guy so be it."

"Well, all I can say is good luck. You have to do what you have to, to make yourself happy. But you are just about to open up a volcano that's already about to erupt. Are you sure you can handle it?'

"I don't know. I'll let you know after it happens. I'll let you go. I'm sorry I woke you."

"I'm not. Just be careful Tyler. I love that girl and if you do anything to make her life more miserable than it already is you'll have me to answer to."

"I'll make you a promise. I won't come back without her. That's how determined I am to win her back."

"Take care and keep in touch."

"Thanks. I'll call you again in a few days, bye." Hanging up the phone, he grabs another beer.

Chapter Seventeen

Awakening the next morning Samantha hears the ocean from the open sliding glass door. Rolling over she notices Brian isn't in bed beside her. Sitting up, she wraps the same sheet around her and walks over to the balcony but Brian's not there either. Walking towards the bathroom she sees a note laying on the little round table. Opening it she reads.

Samantha:
Yesterday and last night were wonderful. I had a few things to take care of early this morning and I didn't want to awaken you. I don't know what you have planned for today, but as soon as I'm finished I'll call you. If you're not there I'll leave a message and catch up with you later. Always,
Brian

Samantha doesn't quite know what to make of the note, because as far as she knows he's done with his media sales meetings and has today free before he flies to Chicago tomorrow. She thought he wanted to spend as much time with her as he can before he has to leave.

Putting Brian aside she decides to shower, go down to the hotel café for breakfast then soak up a few rays before he calls. She's started a new book that she's enjoying and will read some while she's at the pool.

She's towel drying her hair as she comes out of the bathroom and walks over to turn the TV on for the morning news. Walking towards the TV she notices a folded piece of paper on the floor. Reaching down she picks it up and is examining it on her way back up. She doesn't remember seeing it lying on the table or night stand since she's been here. "Hm, wonder what this is?" she asks herself out loud, unfolding the paper. On it appears a name and phone number that reads: Rebecca 437-2172. Her heart starts pounding. Thinking to herself it has to be Brian's, because it isn't hers. It must have dropped out of his pocket. She's wondering why he'd have it in his bathrobe anyway? Was he wearing it when she gave him the phone number? She's now wondering if he's who he says he is. She's starting to panic.

Putting the paper in her purse, she starts wondering who Rebecca is? They really hadn't discussed his life; it was mostly Todd's tragedy. She's wondering if this is a girlfriend, wife or possibly someone he's met while at the convention.

She pulls her wet hair back into a ponytail and puts on her bathing suit. She doesn't feel much like eating anymore and decides to bypass breakfast and head for the pool.

Once there she finds a chaise far away from anyone else so she can be alone. But reading isn't what she's able to do. She can't get her mind off of the name and phone number. She can't believe she's been so stupid to fall for this guy but she has and it hurts. But at the same time she wants to give him the benefit of the doubt until he has a chance to explain. She's wondering where he is and what he's up to? Could he be with her right now?

After he's finished his breakfast Tyler makes his way down to the pool to soak up a little sun. He notices Samantha lying on her stomach in a chaise and fortunately has her back to him. He's able to pick a chaise where she can't see him but he can see her. He'd like nothing better than to approach her but he feels the timing isn't right. He wants to watch her a while longer.

After about a half hour Samantha rolls over and sits up in the chaise. Tyler can see from where he's at that she's crying and becomes very concerned. She reaches in her beach bag for something to wipe her eyes and her cell phone rings. But he's too far away to hear what she's saying.

Samantha answers her ringing cell phone knowing more than likely who's on the other end.

"Hello."

"Samantha, is that you? I can hardly hear you."

"It's me."

"I'm back in my room. Where are you?" he asks sarcastically.

"I'm at the pool. Brian, we need to talk can I come up?"

"What's wrong? You sound upset."

"No. I'm on my way up. I'll be there in a few minutes." She gathers up her book, lotion and water bottle and puts them into her beach bag.

Tyler observes what she's doing and becomes upset. She's leaving as soon as she disconnects her cell phone. Concerned he gathers up his belongings too, and follows her.

"Samantha, you've been crying. What's wrong?" Brian asks, seeing her face when he opens his door.

Reaching into her beach bag she pulls out the piece of paper. She's glad that at the last minute she decided to bring it with her instead of leaving it in her room.

"What's this?" he asks as she hands it to him. Looking down at it, he knows and his heart sinks.

"Who is she, Brian?"

"I'm so sorry, Samantha!"

"Sorry, sorry about what?" she asks, becoming more suspicious.

"Come here, Samantha," he says reaching for her arm and trying to pull her closer.

"No!" she says, pulling back. "Who is she?" she asks, more persistent.

Almost sick to his stomach he's aware he has to tell her. "Samantha, I'm married."

"*Married!* You son of a bitch! How could you do this to me? I confided in you and told you my whole sad story and you let me fall for you. How could you?"

"That's it, Samantha. You told me your story and I felt so sorry for you, I wanted to be your friend, but instead I'm starting to fall in love with you. Samantha, I haven't had a real marriage for some time now. We haven't gotten along for about a year."

"That's still no reason for you to do this to her or me. Don't you realize what this has done to me? You've made me out to be a fool."

"I'm so sorry, Samantha."

"Don't tell me you have any children, Brian. Do you?"

"No, I don't."

"And should I believe you?"

"Yes, you can believe it, I have no kids. Samantha, will you give me some time? I don't want to lose you."

"No, Brian, I can't give you some time. We're through!" she says and stomps out of his room, slamming the door behind her.

As she's making her way back towards her room tears streaming down both cheeks she can't see her hand in front of her face and runs right smack dab into someone walking towards her. Not noticing whom it is she excuses herself and tries to pass. But as she does so he grabs her arm.

"Samantha what's going on?" Tyler asks, grabbing her arm.

"Let me go!" Samantha screams trying to pull her arm out of his grasp not realizing it's Tyler.

"Samantha it's me, Tyler. Let me help you."

Completely taken by surprise she looks up and sees it's him. "And what the hell are you doing here?"

"I'm here to find you!" he says, not letting loose of her arm.

"I don't need to be found, leave me alone!" she says, pulling her arm out of his grasp.

Tyler fishes his key card out of his pocket, inserts it in the door and the green light appears. "Come in here with me Samantha, we need to talk."

"Like hell we do! I have nothing left to say to you! Our relationship was history a long time ago."

"Samantha just hear me out will you please?" he asks, practically begging.

Out of exhaustion Samantha agrees just to shut him up and to get out of the hallway as other guests are starting to come back to their rooms.

Once inside he goes into the bathroom for tissues for her. Her face is a tear-streaked mess, but through those tears she's beautiful just the same. He's loved her from the get go and this is his last chance to win her back. But, he doesn't want it to be on the rebound from this jerk.

"Samantha what happened?"

"First I want to know how you knew I was here and why you came."

"Okay, sit down. Would you like a soda or a beer?"

"A soda, thanks, it's too early for beer." But she doesn't sit.

"I might as well tell you the whole story from the beginning."

"Yes, that would be a good place to start," she says, feeling a little bit calmer. "But I can promise you it won't get you to first base. I've just about had it with men!"

"Are you going to be quiet so I can tell you or not?"

"I'm listening," she says, taking another drink of her soda.

"I've been working for you at *The Tribune* since Todd died."

"You have not. Lee's covering for me."

"He is right now, yes, but that's only because I'm here. George called me when Todd died and I came down immediately. He assumed you'd take leave for a while and he thought I'd be the best one to cover for you. I wanted to do this for you Samantha!"

"So you were working for me when I saw you at Todd's funeral?"

"Yes."

"Then my parents knew and didn't tell me?"

"No, not then. Your mother found out right before I came here. George and I were having lunch and we ran into her. She was meeting a friend for lunch. George asked if she'd heard from you and she said you'd just called her from Hawaii and mentioned this guy you kept talking about. She's very concerned Samantha. George wouldn't tell me where you were. I was just fortunate enough to be in the right place at the right time. When we got back to work I made George tell me what island you were on. Then I figured the rest out from there."

"Why did you come, Tyler?" she asks as her whole body seems to slump as all the fight goes out of her.

"I was coming anyway if I could find out where you were. Then your mother mentioned this other guy and how concerned she is and here I am. She still doesn't know I was working for you. George felt she would be furious. And as far as I know she doesn't know I'm here now."

"She would be. Go on, why did you come here? It seems I have a lot of time to myself now, so I can listen," and she finally sits on the edge of the bed before her legs give out from under her.

"I almost hate to tell you now with what you've just gone through. I don't want to add to your agony."

"I'm almost numb anyway. Nothing you can tell me can shake me now," she says, staring down at the soda can.

"Samantha, I've never stopped loving you and I think you know that already. The hardest thing I've ever had to do in my entire life was letting you go while I was in the hospital. I did that out of love for you. I didn't want you to have to take care of me the rest of your life." Saying this, he kneels down in front of her.

"That was for me to decide, wasn't it, Tyler?"

"Ultimately, it was, yes. But I knew what your answer would be and I couldn't let you do it. I wanted you to be free. You had too much going for you. I knew you'd find someone that was more worthy of you than me and you did. I understand Todd was a wonderful husband," he says and takes the strand of hair that's fallen over her forehead and slips it behind her ear.

Feeling the tingling that his fingers leave on her forehead, she says, "He was, yes. But we could have had that, too, and you knew it.

"I didn't know that at the time, Samantha. I could have been in a wheel chair for life."

"But you aren't, are you?"

"No, thankfully I'm not. But that's in the past now. When I heard your mother talking about this guy you'd met here I couldn't stand it.

I had to see what you were getting yourself into. It didn't sound like the Samantha I knew that would fall for a guy a few weeks after her husband just died. If you were going to fall for anyone I wanted it to be me." His knees can't take anymore; he gets up and sits beside her on the bed.

"Well, it's over now. I just found out he's married," she says, looking up from the soda can and looking him in the eye.

"I'm so sorry, Samantha, but what did you expect? This is a guy you just met that's at a convention for crying out loud. Do you know anything about him at all?"

"No, not really. I fell for him and decided to throw caution to the wind. Everyone else I've ever loved has either dumped me or died, so I said what the hell!"

"So you decided to have some fun, was that it?" He's shaking his head in disbelief of what he's hearing.

"Yes, that just about sums it up. What did I have to lose?" She could feel the life draining right out of her body.

"A lot if you think about it." But he knows rationalizing is not what she's been doing.

"I didn't think about it. I didn't really care anymore," she says, setting the soda can on the floor and putting her face in her hands. "Tyler, I'm tired. I've been through enough."

"What a way to have a good time.," he says, shaking his head.

"No, not a way to have a good time was it?" she finally asks, looking Tyler in the eye."

"That's the first smart thing I've heard you say since we came in here."

"Tyler, what do you want from me?" she asks seriously.

"I want you, Samantha. You know I love you." Tears well up in his eyes as he makes the statement he's been waiting to have the chance to say since he told her goodbye at the hospital so many months before.

"But, Tyler, I honestly don't know what there is left of me to want. I'm broken and I need to put myself back together before I can do anyone else any good. And right now I don't have a clue of how to begin."

"I can wait." All he wants is a chance. He knows in time he can win her back, all he has to do is convince her. Feeling her hurt, he puts his arm around her shoulders and pulls her close.

"But I can't make any promises," she says, not resisting his pull.

"Let's see how it goes. How soon are you going back home?"

"I still have another two weeks and I'm staying here. It won't do me any good to go now, I'm not ready," she says with a little determination in her voice.

"I'm not asking you to go now. Can I stay here with you?" He's hoping beyond all hope that she says yes.

"I can't make you go back. I want the time alone to think and heal. I can't promise you I'll spend much time with you."

"That's fine. I'll take the time you'll give me. I just want to be here for you if you need me." He takes a hold of her hands in hopes she doesn't pull them away.

"Could get pretty boring." She looks up and there's a hint of a smile on her face.

"Here in Hawaii? I doubt it." He's already thinking of things they can do together.

"I still can't believe I physically ran into you."

"Well, I'm glad you did. Do you think you are through with this Brian guy? Or do you think he'll still try to see you?"

"I'm not sure. I was pretty shocked when I found the paper. He insists he loves me and still wants to see me, but I told him we're through. He's supposed to go back to New York the day after tomorrow, anyway. Maybe now he'll leave a day early."

"I'll be right here if he tries to see you." He has no intention of letting Brian get anywhere near her. When he gets through with him, he'll wish he'd be on the next plane off the island.

"That's another question. How'd you get the room right across the hall from me? They wouldn't have told you my room number."

"No, actually it was an accident. I saw the two of you enter the elevator and I looked to see what floor you were on. When I checked in and they gave me my key card I couldn't believe it was on the same floor. But I must confess, I didn't know what room you were in until last night when I heard a knocking on the door and thought it was mine. When I answered the door it was your room, not mine. I saw him standing outside your door in his boxers, holding a bottle of wine."

"No! You didn't see me did you, Tyler?"

Tyler, shaking his head, confesses. "I must say you looked sexy wearing that sheet."

"Oh my God! I even came out in the hall to make sure no one saw Brian in his boxers and you were watching me!"

"I couldn't stand it, knowing what must have been going on behind that closed door." He mentally sees Samantha standing outside in the hall in that sheet.

"I'm sorry, Tyler."

"That's okay, you didn't even know I was here and I shouldn't have been eavesdropping, but I'm glad I was," he says with a sexy smile on his face.

"You need some much needed rest Sam, you look exhausted."

"I am. I think I'll go to my room now. And you know what?"

"No, what?"

"That's the first time I've been called "Sam" since you threw me out of the hospital that day." It did her heart good to hear it.

"I'm the *only* one who's supposed to call you by that name."

Getting up Samantha gathers up her beach bag and heads for the door when Tyler grabs her and pulls her into his arms. It feels so good to have her there that he doesn't want to let her go. Nothing is for certain and he isn't sure he will ever get her back again.

Samantha can feel the love Tyler has for her as he holds her in his arms. But can she return that love now or ever?

"Get some rest, Sam, and I'll call you in the morning," he says, reluctant to let her go.

"Thanks Tyler," she replies, turning to walk across the hall to her room.

Chapter Eighteen

The next morning Samantha lies in bed for quite a while thinking of everything that happened yesterday. She can't believe Brian is married nor that Tyler's come so far looking for her. "What's happening to my life?" she asks herself. "I'm in Hawaii to get away from my grief and it seems to have followed me here! Why Lord, why me?"

She knows the last thing she said to Brian yesterday was that she didn't ever want to see him again but after some rationalizing she believes it isn't entirely his fault. Tyler was right; she had no business even entering into a relationship on the rebound. Todd hasn't been gone that long and for the life of her she can't believe what she's done.

Getting out of bed she grabs a bottle of orange juice out of her rooms tiny refrigerator, walks over to the sliding glass door opens it and walks out onto her balcony wondering who in their right mind would ever want to leave this paradise. She's making a mockery of her visit here and she should be enjoying every minute of it. Lord only knows when and if she will ever get back this way again.

After much thought the first thing on her agenda today will be to call

Brian and see if he'll agree to meet with her. She obviously doesn't know if this is the smartest thing in the world to do, but she believes she deserves a better explanation of why he did this to her.

Brian is completely blown away when she calls. Of course, he agrees to meet with her and he can't wait to see her.

"Samantha," he says, opening the door when she knocks.

"I'm only here because I feel I need a better explanation of why you didn't tell me you were married," she says, walking in and elects to sit in a chair at the desk rather than risking sitting on the king-size bed. It doesn't look as inviting as it did the day before.

"I want you to believe me when I say I didn't come to this convention to bed you or any woman for that matter. But when I met you on the plane and you started telling me your tragic story I felt sorry for you. I found myself wanting to help erase some of your grief. If I could fill a few of those lonely hours with you here I figured it'd make you feel better. I must admit I get lonely, too. And you were more than willing to let me do so. I didn't expect to fall in love with you Samantha. My marriage has been a shambles for quite some time. We married young before we really knew what love was."

"I'm not blaming you for all of this, Brian. After I flew out of your room yesterday I ran into an acquaintance."

"Oh, and who was that?"

"Remember me telling you about Tyler?"

"Wasn't he the guy working on the murder case that you fell in love with?"

"One and the same. He just happens to be in the room right across the hall from me and when I ran out of your room there he was."

"What the hell is he doing here?"

"Looking for me. He ran into my mother in a restaurant back home and she was telling my boss that I kept mentioning you. He became very concerned and I think even a little jealous."

"How do you feel about that?"

"I don't know. But I explained what happened and he more or less said I'd asked for it. He said I fell for you on the rebound and that you weren't totally to blame. That still doesn't excuse the fact though that you are married. How far were you going to let this go before you told me you were married?"

"When I left yesterday morning and left you the note I was trying to convince myself that I needed to tell you, but I didn't want to lose you. Rebecca had called and the guilt was taking over. She'd given me the phone number of a friend she'd decided to stay a couple days with. I'd left it in my robe pocket and you found it. I'd decided to tell you before I left to go back to NY. I knew of course I'd lose you, but I felt it was the right thing to do. I don't know that I want to resolve our issues with my wife but that's something I'll deal with when she gets home. If and when we do divorce would it be okay if I contact you?"

"No, Brian, that won't be a good idea." She's shocked that he can even ask.

"Are you going to go back to Tyler?" he asks, disappointed that she won't consider seeing him again.

"I don't know what I'm going to do. He's hurt me, too. Right now I just want to remain here and salvage the rest of my trip. Of which I'm going to start right now. I need to go." And she starts walking towards the door.

"I'm really glad you came back to see me Samantha. I hope sometime that you can find it in your heart to forgive me," he says, following her to the door.

"They say time heals all wounds. We'll see. I've got a lot of healing to do." She opens the door and starts out. "Goodbye, Brian."

"I'll never forget you, Samantha," Brian says to her as she's walking out.

Chapter Nineteen

Samantha's returned to her room and is sitting on the bed contemplating whether she actually wants to stay and salvage the rest of her trip or just return to Palmetto. At this point she doesn't foresee that she has anything left there either. Sure her parents and her job are there but what else does she really have to go back to? Everything she'd hoped for especially her future with Brian is gone. She's sure that if she would go back, Tyler would only follow her. He won't stop until he has a chance to prove to her that he loves her and wants her back.

Night has set in when Samantha awakens. She must have fallen asleep on the bed. She must have slept for a few hours. Turning over, she looks at the clock on the night stand beside her bed. Her stomach is growling; she hasn't eaten since breakfast. It doesn't take but a second to recall what transpired earlier in the day. She rolls over on her back groaning and asking herself, why me. The strong person she is, she decided before she fell asleep that she would stay for the duration of her trip. She knew she needed to and right now the memories back home were still too fresh. Maybe she could make more sense of things if she just stays and lets the remainder of her trip play out. She knows she probably won't be able to avoid Tyler, but she'll deal with him when and if the time comes. He's come all this way so he should enjoy his stay also.

She showers and dresses for dinner. She's decided on a khaki pair of slacks and black camisole. Picking up her purse from the corner table she turns off the TV opens the door and exits. As she turns to double-check that the door is securely locked she glances across the hall and notices a light in under Tyler's door. She'd momentarily forgotten he was directly across from her. She catches herself wondering what he's doing right now but knows that she doesn't want to talk to him. It isn't going to be easy staying here if he's here also.

Her meal of steak and shrimp hit the spot. Her plate is cleaned and she's full. She can't believe that she actually finished the whole meal. When they'd brought it to her table she was sure she couldn't finish it and she'd told the waitress as much. As she pays the tab and tips the waitress she feels the warm breezes come through the open front door of the restaurant. It's such a warm night she decides to take a walk on the beach. Many a night at home she and Todd would walk the beach after their evening meal. It was sort of their dessert, no calories either. She bends down to take off her sandals to let the sand get between her toes. She can hear the music coming from the different resorts as she walks along close to the water. The lights dance on the water to give light along the way as the foam trickles to shore falling over her feet. It feels cool and refreshing.

Seeing the pier off in the distance she decides to walk to it. It isn't that far and there seems to be a lot of people out tonight and she feels safe. The waves in Palmetto are nothing like here. A person wouldn't even think of surfing there unless a major storm was on the horizon and they still wouldn't compare anything to the size of them here. She makes a mental note to come out tomorrow and watch them surf. It fascinates her to watch.

Climbing the steps to the pier she notices there are still quite a few people fishing. As she heads for the farthest point she watches as different ones are taking their catch off their hooks while making small talk to whomever is standing next to them. Everyone seems to be relaxed and having a good time. Being distracted by watching the fishermen she doesn't realize that she's being watched. She doesn't see Tyler leaning on the side of the pier watching every step she makes towards him.

With her head turned her attention is on a father showing his son how to bait his hook when she feels this hand on her forearm. Turning Tyler stops her before she runs smack dab into him not realizing she's reached the end of the pier.

"Oops, I'm sorry," she says, but is not looking up.

"Better watch where you are going young lady," The voice says. "Or you'll be taking a long walk off of a short pier."

The voice sounds very familiar and as she turns she sees that it's him. "Oh! I guess I wasn't paying attention was I? Hello, Tyler." She wasn't expecting to run into him knowing that when she left her room his light was on.

"Nice evening," he remarks, taking his hand off of her arm.

"It's beautiful. That's why I decided to take a walk. I enjoy it so much back home when the evenings are like this."

"Don't you know it's not safe to be out here alone?" He immediately notices the black camisole she's wearing and worse yet; he knows exactly what's under it.

"There's such a crowd out here I figured I'd be just fine." She can feel his eyes on her even though it's almost completely dark.

"Want to take a walk?"

"I've just been on a little walk, but I guess I could walk some more." The evening breezes feel so good on her skin and she's really not ready to return to her room just yet. "How am I supposed to get my thoughts together when the first evening I go out, I run into you?" she asks, turning around walking beside him back down the pier.

"I honestly didn't think you'd be out here this time of night by yourself. I had no intentions of running into you. I couldn't stand the four walls of my room any longer so I decided to come out. You know how much I enjoy the beach in Palmetto."

"By the way, who's covering for you at *The Tribune* while you're here? You're supposed to be covering for me. I'll bet George was beside himself when you told him what your intentions were."

"Sam, you can't imagine what George said to me when I told him what my intentions were. But he knew there was no use trying to stop me, because any effort would be fruitless."

Laughing, she can just hear George giving Tyler the lecture. "You haven't told me yet who's covering for you."

"Lee is. Once I told him that you'd hooked up with this guy you'd just met on the airplane, I had no trouble convincing him I was doing the right thing by coming after you. He wished me luck and hoped I wasn't too late. Now does this convince you we were all worried sick? You should have seen your mother the day she ran into us in the restaurant. She didn't know what to think."

"Poor Lee. He must be going out of his mind to be doing his job and mine."

"I don't think he had a chance to even think. He just knew someone needed to be here for you."

"That was sweet of him, I guess. What does it take to convince you, George, and Lee that I can look out for myself?" she asks, a little irritated.

"And a fine job of it you are doing! Look at the trouble you got yourself into and you weren't even off the plane yet!"

"Okay, I don't need another lecture," she says, pouting with her chin lowered almost to her neck. "Do ya think maybe I'm a little too trusting?" As she's saying this she lifts her chin with a little guilty smile on her face.

Putting his arm around her shoulder, he gives her the look of death. "Don't try to shrug off what you've done. You and I both know I need to put you over my knee and spank you. George, would be the first one to agree with me and you know it!"

"Okay, okay, enough already!" She kicks up the sand with her foot in frustration.

"Which reminds me, I need to call George and let him know how things are going."

"Tell him hi and thank him again for being so patient with me. You know, I really don't know when I'll be ready to go back there, if ever."

"What do you mean, if ever? That's your home, Sam."

"I know, but I have nothing but sad memories there. I'm thinking I need a fresh start."

"Have you spoken to your parents since you first arrived here? You know they must be worried sick about you."

"No. I need to touch base again, but I don't know what I'm going to say to them. And I know they'll start on me about coming back home and I'm just not ready to hear it. They'd never understand if I said I didn't want to come back."

"Duh, what would you expect them to think, Sam? They are your parents and it's your home. But don't judge them till you put it all out there. Maybe they will be more understanding than you think."

"I don't even know what I think about it either. I can't imagine you not going back. Where would you go? And what would you do, Sam?" He's walking beside her with outstretched, questioning arms. He knows he won't let her make any moves without him, but this is throwing him a curve he's not expecting. He's going to have to handle her very carefully or she's gone. He can sense a change in her that he didn't see in her earlier. She's contemplating something and he's got to stay on top of it. He doesn't want her taking off on him. He has this gut feeling from what she's saying that's exactly what she has in mind. She may not even know where yet, but she's going. Too much has happened in such a short time span that she's ready to run from it all. He knows she's been strong through it all, but everyone has his or her limits and she's reached hers. And sad to say he knows he's been the cause of at least a part of it, a big part of it. If it hadn't been for him their wouldn't have even been a Todd in her life to lose.

"I liked Steamboat. Maybe I'll go visit Scott and Tracie. They'd help me find a place to stay."

"Are you kidding me? It's freezing out there! Why would you want to go back there? You're a fair weather girl." He can't believe this is coming out of her mouth. He wonders if she even really knows what's she's saying.

"I know. I just wanted to hear your reaction!"

Grabbing her arm he turned her to face him. "Don't ever say those things again. You are scaring me Sam. Promise me you won't do anything stupid!"

"I won't. But, I can't promise that I'm going back to Palmetto. I'm serious when I say I don't know if I'll ever be ready."

"It's getting late and we've walked farther than both of us thinks. Are you ready to go back?"

"Oh my gosh!" Looking back she can barely make out their hotel in the distance. It's so dark now that the only thing distinguishing it from all the others lined up on the beach is the neon sign on the building's side. "How far do you think we've walked?"

"No matter how far we've walked, we still have that far to walk back. Let's go." He takes her hand, turns her around and they head back.

Approaching their hotel they both feel as if they've walked miles, which indeed they've walked a good two. Samantha's grateful that she's had this time with Tyler. At the same time, he's glad that she's allowed him this time with her. Samantha loves the sounds of the Hawaiian music she hears coming from the hotel.

"Hey, sounds like we're just in time. Would you like to have a drink and maybe dance a little?" Tyler asks as they reach the top row of steps leading to their hotel.

"Are you kidding me? After where we've just walked?" Samantha's out of breath just reaching the top of the stairs.

"You wimp! Okay, how about a drink first then we'll think about that dance?" He's laughing at her knowing that after the drink he's pretty sure he can talk her into that dance. There's nothing more he'd like than to get her in his arms on the dance floor. He's waited a long time for this and he doesn't plan on waiting too much longer, whether she's aware of it or not.

"Fine, a drink it is. I am thirsty. Order me a Mai Tai will you? I'm going to the restroom. I'll be right back."

"Sure. I'll find us a table." He heads for the bar as she excuses herself for the restroom. He doesn't see any empty tables, but there are a couple stools up at the bar, so he sits on one and saves the other one for her.

Upon returning from the restroom, she spots him sitting at the bar and walks up to him. "No tables, huh? This will do just fine." She puts her purse on the bar, sits down, and picks up her Mai Tai.

"How's your drink?" He'd given her a couple minutes to relax and enjoy it before he asked. He's also hoping she's enjoying the music because he fully intends to ask her to dance.

"Great! I haven't had one of these in a long time." She's enjoying the drink and the music immensely. The band's playing an old Hawaiian love song.

"Would you care to dance?" He's hoping like hell that she doesn't turn him down, but he knows he's going out on a limb.

"Tyler, would you take no for an answer?" She's smiling at him, knowing full well that she's going to say yes.

"Absolutely not!" He steps down off his bar stool and takes her hand to help her off hers and he leads her to the dance floor.

He can't believe that this is actually happening. He puts his arm around her waist not holding her too close at first, knowing she could pull back. The song is beautiful and so is she. This is the first time they have ever danced together. He's hoping that it's the first of many new beginnings for them.

Samantha is enjoying their first dance. She has very mixed emotions when it comes to Tyler. She remembers loving him so much and him throwing that love away. She doesn't want to get caught up in the moment and the place and wish she hadn't. Their walk on the beach brought back so many great memories of back in Palmetto. And now here in Hawaii in his arms with this music playing, it could be so easy to going back to the way it was. But would it be right and for all the right reasons? Or would she just be getting caught up in the moment? So many what ifs.

Tyler tightens his arm around her and lays his cheek against her forehead. She doesn't pull away. For that he is thankful. He's hoping the music will never stop and he can hold her like this forever. Pulling his cheek away, he kisses her on the forehead and awaits her reaction.

She's enjoying the music and when he lays his cheek on her forehead it feels comforting. She needs it and finds it welcoming; however, when he kisses her forehead she wants to pull away, but doesn't. He doesn't deserve to be rejected. After all, he's come all this way for her. Yes, he's hurt her, but he's trying to make it right. She won't pull away from him. She knows she still has feelings for him, but it's going to take time. Right now, time's what she has plenty of.

They're playing the last song of the night and Tyler and Sam are still dancing. The lead singer has quit singing and comes down from the stage and taps Tyler on the shoulder. "Sir, this will be our last song for the evening."

Looking up, Tyler nods. "Thanks for letting us know." Looking around, they are the only two left in the lounge. "I guess we're the only ones left."

"Oops." Samantha looks around Tyler's shoulder and smiles back up at him.

"Want to go back out to the tiki bar by the pool for a nightcap, or are you ready to call it a night?"

"A nightcap would be nice." She realizes she's not quite ready to call it a night.

As soon as the music stops they both approach the lead singer and the rest of the band, shake their hands and thank them for their great music. They receive nods from the band members and head outside. The breeze outside has cooled it down to where it's comfortable and it's obvious a number of other vacationers are taking advantage of it because there are only a few seats available at the bar.

"Not too many seats out here either, Sam."

"That's okay, why don't you get us a drink and we'll drink them down by the water?"

"Are you sure? It's getting awfully late."

"That'll be fine. I'm on vacation, remember? I don't have a curfew."

"Okay, wait here and I'll be right back."

In the meantime, she's reflecting back on her evening with Tyler, what it means to her and what he must be thinking about now. She didn't plan on running into him at all this evening and, least of all, spending any time with him. She wanted time to get herself back together after what she'd been through with Brian. After all, in the beginning, this vacation was to mourn Todd and get a direction in her life. And here she is not two weeks later, through another guy and back with one who dumped her at the hospital a little over a year ago. Dear God, Samantha, what are you doing to yourself?

She's rubbing her arms when Tyler comes back with their drinks. "Are you getting cold?"

"Just a little chill ran through me. I'm fine. Thanks for the drink. Let's walk down to the water."

"You really do love the water, don't you? I've never known anyone obsessed with it like you."

"That's why I bought my house by the ocean in Palmetto. I grew up by it and I'm fascinated. However, I don't underestimate it dangers. It can be both breathtaking and dangerous."

They both enjoy their drinks and pretty much sit in silence, but it's getting pretty late and Tyler knows Sam's getting tired. He's caught her yawning a couple times during their conversation. "Sam, I think it's time I take you back to your room. Are you ready to head back?"

They'd sat down on the sand to finish their drinks. As she picks up her sandals, Tyler steps in front of her and offers his hand to pull her up off the sand. She takes his hand and as he pulls her up she loses her balance. In doing so, she falls back onto the sand and pulls him down, also. Trying not to land on top of her full force, he lets go of her hand and both of his hands straddle either side of her. He manages to keep his full weight from falling on her, but he doesn't completely break his fall. It happens so fast she doesn't have time to roll away from him. He lands on top of her and they come face to face with a thud.

"Sam, are you okay?" he asks, having a hard time getting the words out.

"I think so." Her breath is taken away a little, also.

After a few seconds, Tyler realizes the position they are in and relaxes on top of her. He sees that she's okay and he's going to take advantage of the situation. Taking his hand, he brushes her hair away from her face. Looking in her eyes, he leans down and gently kisses her.

At first he doesn't feel her returning the kiss, but a couple seconds later she responds and he doesn't pull back. Their kiss deepens. Neither one of them realizes where they are, nor that there are obviously other people nearby.

He's holding her so tight now, it feels like he might squeeze her to death. It feels so good to have his arms around her. She knows she's never really fallen out of love with him. Even after he practically threw her out of the hospital, then she married Todd. She's always had feelings for him. He'd come into her life at a very difficult time and he put his life on the line for her. She's never forgotten it and never will. But is the timing right now? With all of these feelings going through her, she just knows she doesn't want to let go.

Tyler's waited a long time to have her back in his arms again and this time he doesn't plan on letting her go. The feel of her under him brings back so many memories that his eyes begin to water.

Samantha sees the tears. "Tyler what's wrong?"

"Nothing."

"Nothing, my eye!"

"Do you know how long I've waited to hold you like this again? I honestly never thought I'd get the chance!"

"There has been a lot of water over the dam hasn't there? Who would have thought this much would have happened and we'd be where we are today? Tyler, I can't promise you anything. I don't know where my life's headed right now."

"I know that. But it is a start, isn't it?"

"It's getting late. I think I'd better be going in." She needs to put some space between them before it goes any further and now's the time to do it. She nudges him to push him off her.

"Yes, I know, it's getting very late." He pushes himself up off of her and extends his hand to once again attempt to help her up. This time it works. They both brush the sand off their clothes before heading into the hotel. He's not happy that she didn't give him an answer to his question, but he'll have to wait. At least this is a start and he can hope that there will be more, much more.

Chapter Twenty

Rolling over onto his left side the next morning and looking at the alarm clock on the night stand next to his king-size bed, Tyler can't believe it's going on eleven am. He never sleeps this late. He rolls his head back onto the pillow and rubs the sleep out of his eyes and recaps the night before and his evening with Sam. Smiling to himself he realizes why he slept so late. That was an evening he doesn't want to soon forget. Dangling his legs over the side of the bed he decides to make the effort in getting up.

One of the perks of his room is the ocean view and once again this morning he enjoys it when he opens the curtain, but this morning it takes on a whole new look. He remembers last night and his walk on the beach with Sam, their talk and their kiss. The smile he had on his face when he went to bed last night is returning again this morning.

He decides to shower before calling her this morning. He promised her space and that's what he intends to give her even though he's wondering where and what's she's doing right now. Would she be sleeping in as he did or was she up and at 'em?

After lingering in the shower and watching a little TV to catch up on what's going on in the world Tyler decides to go down to the hotel restaurant for a bite to eat. It's taking everything he's got not to call Sam but he decides to give her a little longer. Maybe a little patience is exactly what he needs to show.

His stomach is empty and they are still serving brunch cafeteria style and the spread of food looks scrumptious. He waits for the hostess to seat him.

"Sir, a table for one?" The hostess inquires.

"Yes, please."

"Right this way." And the hostess seats him by a window. "Would you like a copy of the morning paper, sir?"

"Please," Tyler says. "Thank you."

A waitress appears at his table a few minutes later with a paper and is prepared to take his order. "Sir, would you like to see a menu?"

"No, I think the brunch looks great, thank you. I'll just go through the line if that's okay."

"That's fine, anytime you are ready," the waitress says and makes notation of it on her notepad. "Would you care for juice or coffee?"

"Both please. And I take my coffee black."

"Thank you, I'll have those right out."

In the meantime, Tyler goes to the beginning of the line and observes the food that is out for brunch. There are too many things to choose from and he knows that his eyes are probably bigger than his stomach so he tries to pick and choose wisely. He decides to go more for lunch than breakfast since it's getting well past the breakfast hour.

It's disgusting how much food he's managed to consume in such a short time, but it all tasted so good. Looking down at his watch he calculates the time back in Palmetto. He really needs to touch base with George and see how things are going. Plus, he really wants to tell him about his latest development with he and Sam. He knows George will be happy for him.

George's secretary buzzes into his office with Tyler's phone call. She's been told not to bother him for the next few hours unless it's important but she knows he'll want to talk to Tyler and she interrupts him anyway.

"George?"

"Teresa, this had better be important?"

"It's Tyler. I thought you might like to take it."

"Hell, yes, I want to take it. Which line is he on?"

"Line four."

"Thanks, darlin'."

"You're welcome," and she gives him the call.

"Tyler, how the hell are you?" George is so glad to hear from him.

"Fine, George, just fine. The weather here's a little warmer than in Palmetto right now but not much. How are things going back at the office? Is Lee hanging in there or about to run out on you?" The waitress is clearing off his table as he's talking to George.

"He's meeting himself coming and going right now trying to do his job and your job or Samantha's job, who's ever job it is." He's shuffling papers on his desk as he's talking to him.

"I know, I know. He must really be getting frustrated."

"I keep telling him to just hang in there it won't be much longer, but jeez, Tyler, how much longer is it going to be? I can't keep telling him this much longer! How's Samantha? Have you had a chance to talk with her yet?" He has so many questions he wants to ask.

"Whoa, George, one question at a time. I'm hoping it won't be too much longer. Tell Lee thanks and I'm doing the best I can. George, I've talked with Sam a great deal and I believe I've made some headway. We were together last night and I really think there are still feelings there." He smiles to himself as he remembers last night and falling down on top of her. If he could only repeat it all over again.

"You telling me boy that she may still have some feelings for ya?"

"That's what I hope I'm telling you, yes!"

"Jesus Tyler, don't blow it!" George is grinning from one ear to the other. He's waited a long time for this as he's blamed himself for a lot that has happened between he and Samantha. Any happiness that they could get would please him.

"I won't, I can promise you that. Have you talked with her parents lately? She told me last night that she was going to call them.

"As a matter of fact I talked with her dad this morning. I saw him at the coffee shop and she had just called them this morning. Funny though, he didn't even mention her saying anything about being with you."

"Think about it, George. They aren't that crazy about me, remember?"

"Yeah, right! You aren't their favorite person are you? But under the circumstances you did make a flying trip over there to make sure she was all right. They should give you some slack."

"You'd think they would, wouldn't you?" The waitress returned wanting to know if he wanted any more juice or coffee and he made a no motion with his hand and a no shaking his head back and forth.

"What did he say she said?"

"He thought it was really strange. She said something about not being ready to come home yet and didn't know when or if she'd ever be ready. He said they both thought she was acting a little strange, but that they couldn't put their finger on it. I'll bet it was you and she didn't know how to approach the subject knowing how they feel about you."

"Gee, thanks." He's a little more curious right now knowing how she felt last night. He doesn't think it has anything to do with him. He's thinking more about what she'd said earlier and not being ready to go back to Palmetto and if she'd ever be ready.

"George, I'm going to be honest with you. Earlier last night before we'd really had a chance to talk about *us*, I'd mentioned something to her about going home and her parents being worried about her. She in turn told me she wasn't ready to go home and didn't know if she'd ever be ready to return to Palmetto. I encouraged her to call her parents, which I guess she did do, but it sounds like I didn't get through to her about returning home." He's wringing his hands in his napkin now wishing he'd called her when he'd first gotten up this morning. Looking at his watch it's already past one.

"I'm getting worried about her. I thought things were really good between us when I walked her back to her room last night George. In fact I know they were. I promised her some space, so I didn't call her

when I got up this morning. God knows I wanted to, but I refrained."
He's already headed out of the restaurant and into the lobby.

"Tyler, keep your cool. Don't make more out of this than you should." He's scratching his head and wondering if he should have kept his mouth shut.

"I'm going to call her right now. I have this gut feeling and I don't like it. I hope she's either in her room or I can find her out by the pool or down on the beach sunbathing. Something tells me I should have done what I wanted to do and called her when I first woke up this morning. I'll call you just as soon as I've talked with her."

"Tyler, I hope your gut feelings are wrong. You call me just as soon as ya know something, ya hear?" By now George is just as worried as Tyler and his stomach is rumbling from too much greasy food at lunch at the local diner.

"You'll be the first to know after me. Don't forget to talk to Lee for me. We'll talk soon." He hangs up. He heads for the nearest house phone to call Sam's room.

The phone rings and rings. No one answers.

Chapter Twenty-One

Samantha can't believe she's slept as soundly as she has and this is the first morning in a long time that she's woke up with a smile on her face. If anyone had told her she would have spent last night with Tyler she would have had to call him or her liars. She thought those feelings were long buried and gone. But did she really or did she just think they weren't ever going to be a reality ever again. So much water over the dam.

She'd sat up long after Tyler walked her back to her room last night. In fact it'd been till the wee hours in the morning. She had a lot of thinking to do about where she wants to go from here. She's made one decision for sure and that is she wants some time alone without Tyler to see if her feelings last night are for real. She needs to get away by herself where he is nowhere around. She knows he will be furious and will no doubt come looking for her but with any luck at all he won't look where she's going right off and will give her a few days alone. She knows he'll start looking in Colorado first. She'd pretty much planted that seed last night.

Calling her parents isn't going to be easy so she decides to get it out of the way before she even takes a shower or starts to pack. She's mentally calculating the time difference and makes the call. Her dad answers. "Hi, Dad, how are ya?"

"Samantha, is that you? I can hardly hear you." He's straining, trying to hear.

"Yes, Dad, can you hear me better now?" She goes out onto her balcony to get better reception on her cell phone.

"Fine, dear. How are you?"

"I'm fine, Dad, and how's Mom?" A few tears well up just hearing his voice and she wipes them away with her fingers.

"She's fine. She's standing right here. Is everything going all right now? Is that guy bothering you anymore?" He's so concerned but doesn't want to sound overly protective.

"He's gone, Dad, and everything's fine."

"Honey, your mother wants me to ask how soon you're coming home?" He's waiting for an answer, looking into her mother's eyes.

"I don't know, Dad. I've got some things to sort out and I don't know where I'm going or what I want to do." She's already afraid she's telling them too much and all she wants is to be alone.

"I just want the two of you to know that I'm okay and I'm doing just fine. Please don't worry. I know you will anyway, but please trust me, I know what I'm doing, okay?" Looking out over the balcony she's hoping that this will ease their minds, but at the same time she knows that they will only worry.

"Keep in touch, get some rest and when you get back maybe you can put all of this tragedy behind you. Your mother sends her love, we both do." He gets the sense that she wants to keep this conversation short and their connection isn't the greatest and he doesn't want to get cut off.

"I love you both and I'll call soon." Hanging up, she feels their love, but she isn't going home. Not yet anyway. She heads for the shower.

In the shower she tries to put the conversation with her parents behind her. It only makes her homesick and she won't go there. She can't go home, not yet anyway. If she does her life will just pick up where she left off and that's what she doesn't want. She wants a fresh start. There are too many sad memories there and her parents are just going to have to understand. She's sure they will once she's made the decision herself in what she wants to do, where she wants to do it and with whom she wants to do it with. If Tyler works in the equation is still unknown. This she still has to figure out.

It's noon and she still has a few things to throw in the suitcase. If she's not careful she won't make her flight nor get out of here before Tyler contacts her. She's already surprised that he hasn't called. He knows she wants her space but last night he was thrilled to have a little time with her. She can't believe that he's being true to his word, but she's glad this one time that he is.

There's a knock at the door and she catches her breath. She hopes it's not him. She looks through the peephole in the door and sees the bellhop standing outside. She'd called for one to get her luggage. Answering the door she lets him in, but asks him to wait a second. He has to smile because she walks over to her luggage and has to practically sit on it to get it shut.

"Miss, would you like for me to get that for you?" he asks, pointing at the piece of luggage.

"Thanks, would you mind?" she asks, embarrassed and a little red-faced.

He walks over and manages to shut it and gets it zipped. Looking over on the dresser, he sees other luggage. Would you like for me to take that too, Miss?"

"No, thanks. I'm leaving that here. I'll be returning. I'm only going for a few days.

"Fine, I'll take this down for you then. Your taxi is here to take you to the airport. Can I tell them you will be down soon?" He has the luggage on the cart and is ready to leave.

"Yes, I'll be right behind you. I just want to make sure I have everything." She hands him a few dollars tip. Looking around, she doesn't see anything else that she will need with her, so she picks up her purse and heads for the door. She feels her pocket to make sure that her room key card is in it. She wants to stop by the desk before she leaves to let them know when she will be returning and to make sure that her room will be safe while she's gone.

Once she's checked at the desk and they've assured her that everything will be fine while she's gone she heads for the waiting taxi to take her to the airport. She doesn't realize that in the process she just misses Tyler leaving the restaurant as he hangs up talking to George before he calls her room to check up on her.

Samantha arrives at the airport none too early. She barely has time to check her flight on one of the airport monitors and notices that it's leaving on schedule and she needs to hightail it to the ticket counter. Any other time her flight would be delayed and she'd have to wait, but not this time. She shouldn't have dillydallied around so long this morning. She's paying for it now.

"Flight 7206 to Maui at one thirty-eight is boarding now. All passengers need to board at gate number four now." Samantha hears them calling the flight, picks up her pace and is about to the ticket counter.

"May we have your ticket please miss?" Samantha pulls it out of her purse as the attendant's asking for it. They're bringing her name up on the computer and printing her boarding pass.

"I'm sorry I'm late," she says, a little frustrated.

"Don't worry, you still have a few minutes," the attendant assures her. "They won't take off without you." She smiles and hands Samantha her boarding pass. "Have a nice flight."

"Thank you," Samantha replies, accepts her boarding pass and hurries for the gate pulling her carry on behind her.

Once aboard the plane she can finally begin to relax. It's such a short flight to Maui; it's hard to believe the trouble you have to go through. You'd think you were going to fly half way across the US. Of course it's no one's fault but her own that she brought so many clothes. But she's not sure how long she's going to stay. It could be a few days; it could be a couple weeks. She's not going back until she has things figured out. Of course the room back on Oahu is costing her a pretty penny to hold but she feels it's worth it.

It is a beautiful flight from Oahu to Maui and Samantha can't wait to get to her hotel. She'd put her trust in the hotel in Oahu to make her reservations for her so she's anxious to see where they've put her. They've also rented her a car and once she's retrieved her luggage she makes her way to the rental counter to pick it up. She's pleased that they've rented her an economy size car. She doesn't plan on going too many places but wants it available if she decides to take some side trips. She's heard that on Maui you need a car to get around but you can only go so far with a rental car because of the rough roads and insurance only covers you traveling so far.

She has no problem getting the directions to her hotel and drives there without getting lost. But by the time she arrives she's exhausted. The bellman retrieves her luggage from the trunk and tells her where she can park the car. They would park it for her but she feels more comfortable doing it herself, therefore will know where it is.

Upon check-in she finds that they have her booked in an oceanfront villa, which she finds quite satisfying and can hardly wait to see it. Once the young gentleman that waits on her at the counter has had her sign all the necessary papers and she gives them her credit card she's ready to follow the bellman to her villa. He leads her back out the front door where they board a golf cart for him to take her to it.

She can't believe her eyes, her own private villa. The bellman opens the door with the key card and steps back for her to enter first. He wants her to get the full view of what she's about to see. From the front door straight through to the ocean she has an unobstructed view. It's absolutely breathtaking. She may never want to return to Oahu much less to Palmetto. Turning around she tells the bellman how breathtaking it is. It's not as if he hasn't heard these exact words a thousand times before. Retrieving her luggage he sets it inside the door. She tips him graciously and he leaves her to her privacy. Walking to the sliding glass door she slides it open and walks out onto the lanai to find the garden patio just as breathtaking as the first view. It reminds her of the setting Julia Roberts had on her garden patio at the end of the movie Pelican Brief. There was a chaise lounge, side table, four chairs and a table all for entertaining if she so desires. But not now, she is ready for solitude. She has to admit she wishes Tyler was here to enjoy it with her.

It doesn't take her long to change into a pair of shorts and a tank top. She's ready for a walk on the beach. Before she goes she opens the door to her room refrigerator and pulls out a bottle of water to drink on her walk. She's wondering if there is anything that she doesn't have. Deciding to go to the restroom before heading out, in closing the door she finds a terry cloth robe hanging behind it. Wow, she says to herself. She thinks this is really neat and looking at the tub she notices it's a Jacuzzi tub. She's going to be treated like a queen.

Once out on the lanai she decides she's more tired than she thinks. She's going to sit on the chaise and take in the view.

Something startles her and she awakens not knowing where she is. Looking around she gets her bounds and remembers she's in her villa in Maui and she once again smiles. Looking at her watch she must have fallen asleep and she's been asleep a couple hours. This must really be secluded because she hasn't heard a thing until now. Getting up she walks towards the ocean and she notices that the nearest villa is at least a hundred yards from hers and there's very dense vegetation between them. She really does have her privacy.

Chapter Twenty-Two

Tyler is very worried when he can't reach Sam in her room and decides to go up and see if he can raise her. Taking the elevating it doesn't get to their floor fast enough to suit him, but when it reaches their floor he hurries to her door and knocks rather loudly but she doesn't answer it either. "Damn, why didn't he call her when he got up this morning? To hell with her space!"

He tries to catch the elevator before it goes back down but without any luck and he has to wait for it to come back up. He keeps pushing the button, but knows it won't hurry things up. Once it does come back up it seems like an eternity before he's back to ground level. When the doors open he wants to check out everywhere on the hotel grounds to see if he can find her. His inner voice tells him that he won't find her but he's going to check everywhere first.

He looks everywhere, but no Sam. That means the beach, restaurants, pool, gift shop, spa, lounge, hair salon and anywhere else he can think of. She's nowhere around. He's afraid she's gone. His next stop's going to be the front desk.

At the front desk he knows the routine and it's exactly what he gets. "I'm sorry I can't give out that information."

"Can I speak to the manager please?" Tyler politely asks the young lady behind the counter. He truly has no patience whatsoever but he knows getting upset will get him nowhere fast.

"Yes, sir. If you'll wait here I'll get him." She leaves him at the counter and goes behind the wall into an inner office to get the manager.

The manager follows the young lady out. "Sir, the young lady here explained your situation to me. I'm sorry, but hotel policy is that we cannot give out the whereabouts of our hotel quests as we'd give you the same courtesy if someone would ask about you."

"I know, sir, and I appreciate that, but I have a feeling that's she's left the island and has headed inland. I'm very concerned about her."

"Have you contacted any of her family? Wouldn't she have let them know if she'd changed her plans?"

"I talked with her boss this morning who in turn had just talked with her parents and she hadn't said anything to them about leaving the island, but they had a feeling that she might do something."

"Sir, she's of age and she's free to come and go as she pleases. I'm sorry there's nothing I can do to help you. If you think there's been any foul play and the police need to be involved then that's another matter. Otherwise I'm afraid I can't release any information. If there's anything later on that I can be of help please let me know."

"Thanks, I'll let you know." He fears she's headed to Colorado like she said last night she might do. But after they'd talked then spent the evening together he'd hoped she'd had a change of heart. He had hopes she had feelings for him. His heart's sinking and his hopes are dwindling.

He decides to call George back because his instincts tell him she's left the island. He doesn't want to call her parents because they either wouldn't believe him or would blame him, so he'd let George handle them. While he's telling them he'd be making reservations to fly to Colorado. If she thinks she's going to get away from him now she has another thing coming. He's gotten this far he isn't backing down now.

George is on the line in a flash. "Tyler what the hell's going on?"

"I can't find her George!"

"What do you mean you can't find her?"

"I've searched this whole resort and she's nowhere to be found."

"Are you sure she's just not out shopping somewhere on the island?"

"No, George, I don't. But after what she said to me last night then this morning to her parents, I have a feeling she's left the island."

"They wouldn't tell me anything at the front desk because I'm not family. Can you call her parents and have them call here and see what they can find out?"

"Sure, I'll call them right now!"

"I'm heading to Steamboat, George. I know that's where she's gone!"

"Steamboat, why would she go to Colorado? It's colder than Hell out there right now!"

"I know, George, but that's where she said she might go. She'd visit Scott and Tracie. They treated her so nice when Todd got killed, she thought she'd return."

"That doesn't make sense."

"Tell me about it! But I'm on my way. If you hear anything from her parents call me on my cell phone."

"Aren't you even going to wait to hear what they find out?" George asks Tyler.

"Nope times a wasting. I can't let her get away from me again George!"

"Tyler, you've lost your mind!" George says for lack of anything else to say to him. He thinks he's going on a wild goose chase this time.

Tyler's made his reservations and is ready to fly off the island in less than two hours. He doesn't realize that he's turned off his cell phone and if George tries to contact him with any news about Samantha he can't get it.

George calls Samantha's parents and they agree to call the hotel in Oahu to see if they will release any information on Samantha's whereabouts and if she's still registered at their resort.

"I hate to have to do this to you after what we have all been through but Tyler is genuinely worried about her."

"We understand George. We both felt like she wasn't herself when she called this morning either. We should have quizzed her more ourselves. Tyler evidently knows her better than we do. And you say he thinks she's headed back to Colorado?"

"That's what he said she mentioned last night when they were together. She needs some space and she thought Scott and Tracie would welcome her and give her the space she needs."

"We don't think that would be the place she needs to go. The tragedy that happened there, couldn't give her any peace."

"Tyler and I agree."

"Well, anyway, we need to get off here and call the hotel. George, we'll call you right back after we talk with them."

"Good luck, I hope they tell you something."

"Us, too. We'll call you right back." He then hung up to call the hotel in Oahu.

Once the call went through to the hotel the same girl that talked with Tyler answered the phone. She couldn't give them any more answers than she gave Tyler, but she got the manager and he talked with them also.

"I'm sorry we haven't been able to be of more help, but we do have hotel policy. I hope you understand this."

"We do, but we are very concerned about our daughter."

After retrieving a little more information from Samantha's parents the hotel manager truly believes they are who they say they are and decides to give them Samantha's whereabouts as far as he knows them. He's already questioned the clerk in what she knows of Samantha's whereabouts before he talked with her parents so he's prepared to tell them.

"I'll give you a little information, but I do wish you'd contact her before you go there to see if she wants you to interfere. We do value our customer's confidentiality and we don't want to lose her as a customer in the future."

"We will be very discreet, we promise you."

"She left here earlier today for a stay on Maui. She kept her room here so she does plan on returning."

"Maui! We thought she left the island for Colorado!"

"Colorado!" The manager says. "Why would anyone want to go to Colorado this time of year? It's dead of winter there now!"

"We know that, but that's where we thought she was headed."

"Can you please tell us what hotel she's staying in on Maui?" her father politely asks.

"Yes, we booked her in a villa at the Marriott. A very nice resort, if I must say so myself. I've stayed there a few times."

"May we have that number?"

He gives Samantha's father the number and he writes it down. "My wife and I want to thank you for all of your help. We know you stuck your neck out in giving us the information you did and we're truly grateful."

"I have a daughter of my own. Good luck and I hope everything works out for you."

Hanging up, they need to get back in touch with George so he can contact Tyler to see if he can stop him from heading to Colorado.

"George, Samantha's still in Hawaii!" Samantha's father relays to George over the phone.

"What? Tyler's headed back to the states as we speak. Where the hell is she?"

"She's not on Oahu, but she did fly to Maui. She's in a villa on the island."

"I've got to try to catch Tyler. I hope I'm not too late. I hate to cut you off but…"

"We understand. You know, we think we were a little hard on Tyler. We may need to rethink our thoughts on him. He truly loves our daughter, doesn't he? He's practically traveled halfway around the world for her."

"Yes, he has. I've kept in contact with him since their accident almost two years ago. He's never stopped loving her and he did what he did because of his love for her. I only hope it's not too late and she sees that sooner rather than later. I don't know how much longer he's going to wait."

"Hopefully, it won't be much longer. That is if he you can catch him before he gets to Steamboat. I'd hate to think what might happen if he gets all the way there and she's basking in the sun in Maui. I know I wouldn't be a happy camper in that situation."

"You two try to contact her and I'll try to reach Tyler. Hopefully, soon we can put an end to all of this with a happy ending. I'll be in touch soon."

"Us, too." Then they disconnect.

George tries Tyler's cell phone several times with no luck. In haste, he must have turned it off by mistake. He decides to call the airport in Oahu to see if he can have him paged before he boards the flight, but he's too late. He misses the flight by about ten minutes. His only hope is that he notices it while he's in flight and turns it back on when he arrives in Steamboat.

He doesn't have Scott and Tracie's phone number so he calls directory assistance and they connect him. Tracie answers the phone but doesn't know George.

"I don't believe you know who I am but I'm George, Samantha's boss in Palmetto, South Carolina."

"Yes, she did mention you when she was here a few months ago. How is she doing? She was really going through hard times when she was here, just losing her husband and all."

"She's been doing okay. That's what I'm calling you about. Did you receive a call from Tyler?" George had no idea whether he even bothered to call them before he left.

"No, we didn't, were we supposed to?"

"He thinks Samantha is with you and Scott right now."

"Good Lord, why would she be here with us?" Thinking to herself she wonders why anyone would want to be in Colorado this time of year when you live in South Carolina.

"No, she isn't here with us. Is she supposed to be?"

"She more or less told him that she was going there to get some much needed space and she thought you and Scott would give her that."

"We most definitely would, if that's what she wants, but she's not here."

"I know that now, but Tyler doesn't. I've been trying to reach him but he evidently has turned off his cell phone and is headed your way."

"Do you know where Samantha is?

"Yes, we do. Her parents found out she's at a resort on the Island of Maui.

"And Tyler's headed here, thinking this is where she is? Boy, isn't he in for a surprise!"

"If this doesn't make him want to break her little neck, nothing will."

"She mentioned him when she was with us after Todd's tragic death. I truly thought she still had feelings for him."

"I always felt she did and he for her. It just never worked out until now."

"Do you think there's a chance for the two of them this soon after Todd's death?"

"I do, yes." Here he goes, trying to play matchmaker again and it's probably going to get him into trouble.

"If it makes them happy then they should go for it. She definitely deserves some happiness in her life. She's been thrown some curves in the last few years."

"When you hear from Tyler will you have him call me?" He proceeds to give Tracie his office phone number. "I'll stay in the office here until I hear from him. And I can guarantee you he won't be a happy camper when he finds out she's in Maui and he's in Steamboat. His trip back won't be a pleasant one and I feel sorry for Samantha when he catches up with her."

Laughing, she wouldn't want to be Samantha. "I'll have him call as soon as I hear from him. Please keep us posted. I can't wait to tell Scott."

It isn't a long flight from Oahu to Steamboat, but of course it is a huge temperature change for Tyler. He, like Sam, prefers the warm beaches versus the snowy mountains. He can't wait to get to Scott and

Tracie's to see Samantha. He has a few choice words for her.

It's very unlikely that he hasn't received a call from George so once he lands he pulls his cell phone out of his pocket and finds that he'd turned it off.

"Damn it!" He disgustingly says to himself. Turning on the phone he does have a message from George but he decides to wait until he sees Sam before calling. This way he can let him know she's okay and he can relate the news to her parents.

Scott and Tracie's isn't a long ride from the airport but it seems like an eternity. He decides to surprise Sam so he doesn't call her to let her know he's coming.

The taxi stops out in front of the Harrison's home and the driver retrieves his duffle bag from the trunk and Tyler tips him before he drives off.

Once he reaches the top step to Scott and Tracie's front door Tyler's already rehearsed what he's going to say to Sam. He rings the doorbell and the door is opened by a beautiful blonde standing on the other side of the threshold but it isn't Sam.

"Hello, is Samantha here?" he asks Tracie.

"No, she isn't. And you must be?" she asks.

"Tyler Wentworth from Palmetto. I thought she was headed this way. Have you heard from her today or maybe even last night?"

"No, we haven't. Were we supposed to?" She's still playing his game but isn't going too much longer. "Would you like to come in? It's pretty cold outside." She steps away from the door and allows him entry.

"Yes, please. I feel I need to explain."

"No explanation needed. I just talked with George. He called and explained and hoped that you were already here. He was wanting to catch you before you left Oahu, but he said you must have turned your cell phone off."

"George called you here?" Tyler's a little more than just frustrated now.

"Yes, he did. He knows that Samantha isn't here in Colorado."

"He does? Then why in the hell didn't he tell me before I flew all the way here? Excuse me for my language. I'm just a little frustrated right now."

"You must not have heard me. He did try to call you several times. You must have turned your cell phone off by mistake."

"I noticed that at the airport. Does George know where Sam is?"

"Yes, he does. Her parents contacted the hotel in Oahu and the manager finally told them where she is staying. George said they are contacting her now."

"Where is she? When I get to her I'm going to break her pretty neck!" He can't believe he's flown all this way and she's not here.

"I hate to be the one to tell you this, but she's in Maui."

"Maui! What the hell is she doing in Maui? There's not much difference between Oahu and Maui!"

"She told them she needed space and the hotel helped her set up this little trip to Maui to be alone."

"Great, I'll have to thank them for this one!"

"Would you like to stay the night with us until you can make flight arrangements to go back? We'd love to have you." She'd love to have a chance to talk to him about Samantha.

"If it wouldn't be too much trouble, I think I will, thank you. I'm pretty frustrated right now and seeing Sam might not be a good idea. Does she know I'm here?"

"I don't even know if she knows yet that her parents are trying to get in touch with her. I'm pretty sure she won't like it the least little bit when she does hear from them."

"She should have thought about that before she went off half cocked to do her thinking. Everyone has been doing their share of worrying about her since Todd's death and her little fling with Brian in Oahu."

"Fling in Oahu! I don't know about this."

"No, I don't know how you could. That's how I ended up in Oahu. If you don't mind I'd like to freshen up then I'd be more than happy to fill you in."

"By then Scott ought to be home from work and you can tell us both at the same time. I'm sure he'll enjoy this also. In the meantime I'll throw something together for us to eat. You just relax for a while."

Tyler enjoys supper with Scott and Tracie and explains the whole episode Samantha had in Oahu with Brian. Neither one of them can believe what Samantha's done.

"Sounds like she needs you," Scott says.

"That's what I'm trying to get across to her and I think that's what she's running from. I truly hurt her and she's afraid I'll do it all over again. I can guarantee you that won't happen. I'm in this time for the long haul and I intend to convince her of it if she'll only give me the time to show her."

"I'll get a flight back to Maui in the morning. I'm not telling anyone I'm on my way. I don't want her to know I'm coming. I'm sure she can guess, but she won't know when. By the time her parents are through with her she'll no doubt be very upset that they won't leave her alone. The last thing she needs is for me to come popping in."

"Do you actually think she'll accept you when you get there?" Tracie asks.

"Yes, I do. And if I have to get down on one knee I'll do that, too. I'm ready for whatever it takes, but I don't think it's going to take much."

"I hope for your sake as well as hers that you are right," Scott says. "She's been through enough."

Tyler's on his cell phone early the next morning and is lucky enough to get a flight out at two in the afternoon Steamboat time. He thanks Tracie for putting up with him on such short notice and promises to call as soon as he can and fill them in on what transpires with him and Samantha.

The ride to the airport is to take about twenty minutes but it's snowing so hard you can barely see the lines on the side of the road and the taxi driver has to slow down to a crawl. It reminds him so much of the weather back home in Pennsylvania. They still manage to arrive at the airport in time and Tyler is relieved to be here. He wouldn't miss this flight. He only hopes now that it's not delayed.

Chapter Twenty-Three

Waking up the next morning Samantha has no idea everyone is looking for her except maybe Tyler and other than being a little annoyed he'll just have to get over it. She's going to enjoy this time by herself starting immediately and spend her first day by calling room service and having a huge breakfast sent over. Looking at the menu she can't believe what choices she has to choose from.

The doorbell rings just as she's coming out of the bathroom tugging on her swimsuit strap. She's making a mental note that while she's here to look for a new suit to replace this old one then she won't have to tackle this disgusting strap anymore.

She opens the door to a bellman with a white tablecloth covered cart filled with silver trays with silver lids and a single red anthurium standing in a bud vase in the center of the cart. She instructs him to take the cart out onto the lanai where she will enjoy her breakfast. He starts to remove the lids from the trays and she stops him and says she's not quite ready, that she'll do it. He nods and asks if there's anything else she desires and she says no. She tips him; he walks back across the room and exits.

Making mental note, her beach towel, sun screen, sunglasses and robe are already laid out on the bed. All she needs is her book and she'd left it on the night stand from last night. She won't need anything out of her room refrigerator until later because she's having juice with her breakfast. Picking everything up she's ready for her day on the lanai and if she's forgotten anything she's only a step away.

Her breakfast of scrambled eggs, bacon, fresh fruit and pineapple muffin is delicious and much more than she can possibly eat. The fruit and muffin she'll keep and eat later, but the rest she's afraid is just wasted. She's enjoying her view of the ocean so much she decides to take a short walk before she gets too relaxed in her chaise with her new book *Palmetto Summer*. Putting on her beach cover up and slipping into her sandals she makes a mental note that a person can get spoiled living like this and the only way she could enjoy this lifestyle very long would be to win the lottery. And a fat chance she'd have of that. Her walk to the water is no more than twenty or so yards. Deciding which direction she wants to walk, she first looks to her left then right. Both ways look about the same, so she decides to go left for no reason other than to just pick one. Lucky for her, or maybe not, she walks towards a little row of shops. A female instinct is maybe the reason she walks left.

There's always this magnet pulling any woman into a shop and Samantha's no different. She's drawn up this little stone walkway to this quaint shop that's full of women's beach clothes; shorts, tops, suits, sundresses, etcetera. She's not exactly dressed to go shopping but everyone around is in beach clothes so she decides to go on in. The salesclerk greets her and asks if there's anything she can help her with and she just smiles back and says she's just looking right now but tells her she has a very nice shop and she'd like to browse a little. It doesn't take much browsing before she finds a white sundress that she absolutely has to try on, but wants to look further in case she finds more and wants to make one trip to the dressing room do the trick. She's not like most women. She'd rather take a beating than try on clothes.

Forty-five minutes later she has her arms full and is ready to tackle the dressing room. The salesclerk unlocks one of the dressing room doors for her and wishes her luck. Trying on the white sundress first she hopes it fits. Looking in the mirror she spins around to see it from the back. She likes how it fits and she's surprised that her first thought is if Tyler will like it? Next she tries on the bright yellow colored two-piece bathing suit. She's tired of wearing the suit she has on with the strap that won't stay up. Once in the suit she's afraid to look in the mirror. It too feels like it fits but one never knows. Putting herself out of her misery she looks in the mirror and has mixed feelings. She can take it or leave it and decides to take it, just because it will replace her old one.

She doesn't take long in trying on the rest of the clothes that she's taken into the dressing room. In addition to the dress and bathing suit she only adds a pair of red shorts and a little white tee shirt to her purchases.

Leaving the shop she's checking the time and can't believe she's been in one shop this long and actually enjoyed it. She hasn't allowed herself leisure like this, she can't remember in how long. There's a fudge shop right next to the shop she's just leaving and her conscious is telling her no, but her sweet tooth is telling her otherwise. She's at the front door and a little bell overhead is ringing before she knows she's even in. Once inside the smell of the fudge is overwhelming and there's no way she's leaving without a slice or maybe even two. Behind the glass encased counters there are more flavors than she can count and making her choice won't be easy. She's used to shops like these being open back in Palmetto during the peak season but she tries to avoid them. She's on vacation and she can't resist. She makes her selections, they're boxed up and she heads back to her villa. She'll save some of the other shops for another day. Taking off her shoes she walks barefoot back to her villa. The ocean here is indescribable in comparison to the Atlantic back in Palmetto and she thought it was awesome until she saw Hawaii.

Her hands are full when she arrives back at the villa as she tries to reach in her pocket for her key to the villa. Putting her packages down on the chaise she's able to retrieve her key out of her pocket and unlock the sliding glass door. Once inside she drops her packages on the bed.

She puts the fudge into the fridge but not before pinching off a small piece of the chocolate walnut.

Holding the sundress up to her and looking into the floor length mirror she wonders where she'll wear it first. She's hoping maybe she'll go out again with Tyler. There she goes again thinking of Tyler. Why can't she get him out of her mind? She hangs the dress up in the closet and takes the rest of her new clothes out of the sack. She decides to put the new bathing suit on and catch some rays.

She spends the better part of the day on the lanai once she returns from her walk and shopping. Her huge breakfast, the leftovers and a little of her fudge gets her through the afternoon. She's read her book, taken a nap and just enjoys the garden around the lanai. It's very secluded and few people pass by. She's spent a lot of time thinking about what she wants to do and where she wants to go from here. She keeps going over her evening in Oahu with Tyler. It was totally unexpected but it's exactly what she needed.

To be needed is exactly what she wants. She wants to put all the trauma and sadness behind her and if she has to leave Palmetto to achieve that then that's what she'll do. She loves her parents dearly, but she has to do what's best for her. It would be tough selling her house on the beach, really tough. She'd gone through so much to get it. She knows George will help her relocate if she wants to stay in investigative reporting, which she's pretty sure she will, but not before giving her fifty reasons why she needs to stay there. Lee would love it because he could step into her position that would be a step up for him and obviously more pay. It's exciting and she never knows from one minute to the next what might happen. She doesn't like repetition, which most jobs come with. Will Tyler fit into the mix; she's not quite sure. It seems in the past whenever she fell in love, him included something tragic happened. Boy does she have a lot to consider.

She decides to call George and run it by him. It's not something she's going to rush in to but she has to start somewhere. They've been so close for a very long time. Looking at her watch he's still at work. Dialing the number direct to his desk she gets his secretary anyway but she puts her through immediately, knowing everyone is looking for her.

Buzzing George, she says, "George. George, Samantha's on line two."

"She's calling here?"

"I guess."

"Put her through." Not knowing what to say, he decides to play it cool and see what she has to say.

"Hi, Samantha, how are you?" he asks a little hesitantly.

"I'm fine. How are you, George?"

"Just fine. Are you enjoying Hawaii?" he asks out of lack of anything else to say.

"Yes, I am. George, I need some advice and you're the only one right now I feel I can confide in."

"You know I love you and I'll help you in any way that I can. Have you talked with you parents lately?"

"Yes, I've talked with them." Knowing full well that they don't know she left the island and she doesn't know George knows.

"How can I help?" He's scratching his head and wondering what she has on her mind.

"What would you say if I want to leave Palmetto and stay in Hawaii?" She knows this is going to be a shock to him.

"Did I just hear you right?"

"Yes, you did. What do you think of the idea?" she asks, half holding her breath for the answer.

"A, I don't want to say anything I'd want to take back later. Samantha, you've really caught me off guard."

"I just want to toss the idea around with you. I really like it here. I know I haven't been here but a few days, but I need a fresh start. I have so many sad memories back in Palmetto, I think a fresh start might be just what I need."

George wishes Tyler would hurry up and get there then he won't have to be in this situation. But he can't tell her and spoil what Tyler's trying to do. "I think my first advice would be to not make any rash decisions right now. You need more time Samantha. Look what you just got yourself into the minute you left Palmetto. You have your leave of absence from the paper for as long as you need it. Take advantage of it, we will be all right. Then if it's still what you want I'll do some searching and see what I can to help you relocate. I don't know anyone personally out there, but I'm sure I have enough contacts that will put me in touch if need be."

"But you don't think I can do it from here now?" She's a little frustrated that he's holding back on her.

"No, Samantha, I don't think you're ready. I think you are running from yourself and you need to slow down. You are no good to anyone right now, most of all yourself. Please try to relax and enjoy your stay there. Don't even think about your work here or your future employment. Can you do that much for me?"

"I guess so, at least I'll try." She's disappointed, but knows he's never given her bad advice in the past.

"Good. Is there anything else?" He's hoping she'll mention Tyler.

"No, I guess not. I know you're busy so I won't keep you. Thanks, George, I love you and I'll keep in touch."

"Love you, too. You try to stay out of trouble and relax, you hear!"

"Yes, I hear, but don't forget about what I asked you. And please don't mention it to my parents when you see them."

"I won't. Bye, Samantha"

"Bye, George." She hangs up, also.

It's early evening and she hasn't any plans. She wishes Tyler were here and they could enjoy the evening together. She's sure there's just as much entertainment here as there was back on the island of Oahu. Breakfast was so tasty; maybe she'll call and have dinner brought out also. After talking with George she's not in the mood to go out.

She finds the menu booklet on the desk and leafing through she tries to decide what to order. The baked tuna, spinach salad with mandarin orange slices and dried cranberries and mixed vegetables are what she decides on. She doesn't have to worry about dessert because she has the fudge she bought this morning in the fridge.

While waiting on her meal to be delivered she opens the bottle of wine she'd gotten out of her own personal locked bar that is in her villa.

She'd unlocked it and put the bottle in the fridge to chill earlier in the day.

Walking out onto the lanai she sits on the chaise to drink her wine and enjoy the view.

Her meal arrives about forty-five minutes later and she's just about out of the mood to eat because she's not feeling well. But everything looks so yummy as the bellman's taking the silver covers off the dishes she doubts she'll be able to leave it be. She tips him then pours herself another glass of wine to have with her meal.

Not feeling any better after she's eaten she showers takes a couple Tylenol and decides to watch a little TV from her bed and give the Tylenol time to work. Channel surfing she stops on the weather channel to see what the weather is like at home in South Carolina. This makes her think of her mom and dad and she begins missing them a little. This isn't good so she immediately changes the channel and tries to find a movie. There's nothing on that she hasn't seen a dozen times so she turns it off and tries to get some sleep.

Sharp pains in her stomach that have her doubled over awaken her suddenly. She's up immediately and into the bathroom vomiting. She's wondering if it was something she ate earlier. But she remembers she didn't feel well before her dinner arrived.

The pain's subsided for the time being and after getting something to drink she returns to bed.

Chapter Twenty-Four

The traveling and worrying about Sam has left Tyler in a lousy mood when he lands on the island but he's still anxious to catch up with her. Of course he's greeted as the other passengers with the traditional lei, which at this point he could care less about but graciously accepts. When he reaches baggage claim the luggage has yet to arrive so he seeks out the nearest bar for a beer to wait its arrival.

He'd had some time on the plane to think about what he's going to say to Sam when he finally sees her. All of the signals were there the other night when they were walking on the beach, that she might leave, but after they'd had that incredible evening he didn't think she'd actually do it. Running after her could make or break their relationship and he knows it. But she's not exactly making rash decisions right now and not only he but also her parents and George know she can't be left alone right now, they don't trust her.

He's decided to do what's best for Sam right now and worry about their relationship later. He has to catch up with her and bring her back where she's safe that is if he can.

He's finished his beer and walks back to baggage claim to retrieve his luggage. There's only one bag still going around on the turnstile and it's obviously his. Grabbing his bag he walks to the nearest exit to see if he can hail a taxi to the hotel Marriott where Sam is staying. He'd already booked a room when he made his flight reservations and he can't wait to check in. All he wants is a hot shower and soft bed which he doubts the hotel will have but there's always hope.

His ride to the Marriott seems to take forever, but he wonders if it just isn't the fact that he wants to get there so bad that it seems longer. The taxi driver pulls up in front of the hotel and retrieves Tyler's bag from the trunk. Tyler tips him, picks up his bag and heads into the hotel.

At the check in desk Tyler gives the lady the necessary information to expedite his check in, but not without noticing how attractive she is. He wouldn't mind getting to know her better if not for being in love with Sam.

Thanking the desk clerk he heads for the elevator to find his room and notices how nice the Marriott is and sees why they set Sam up here. Under different circumstances he wouldn't mind spending a few days here himself. Obviously, others think the same thing because the lobby is packed with tourists. Of course, this is peak season in Hawaii and it's hard to get a room anywhere this time of year. He was lucky to get a room and he probably wouldn't have it had he been a single.

Pushing the door open to his room and sighting the bed first, it looks like heaven. The first thing he should see is the view right in front of him and it isn't the bed. He's been given an oceanfront room and his view is spectacular to say the least. But just like a man all he can see is the bed. Dropping his bag on the floor he takes off his tennis shoes one by one and tosses them under the table by the sliding glass door. Of course the TV remote is the next thing he reaches for and switches it on. Looking at his watch it's almost eight pm. He can't believe it's this late. He's going to wait until morning to find Sam. He's too tired and in no mood. After a shower and a couple beers it's lights out. He's asleep with the TV remote in his hand and the TV's still playing.

It's only six o'clock when he awakens the next morning. He jumps out of bed like he's going to a fire and heads to the shower. He's anxious to see Sam. His big test of the day will be finding out what room she's in.

Food isn't on his mind as he heads for the front desk. The pretty girl that he saw at check in last night was now off duty and the gentleman he was about to approach didn't look like someone he wanted to cross.

"Sir, may I help you?" the desk clerk asks as Tyler reaches the counter.

"Yes, you may," Tyler says as he continues to give him Sam's full name and what his connection with her is.

"I'm sorry, sir, but I won't be able to give out that information."

Tyler's heard this bullshit before and he's not in the mood to hear it again. "Is there anything I can do to get you to release her room number?"

"No, sir, I'm sorry there's not," the desk clerk says and is standing firm. "I can call her room for you if you'd like."

"Yes, would you please so I can speak with her?" He's hoping that she'll talk to him.

Once the desk clerk finds which room she's in he tries to connect to her room, but she's not answering.

"That's strange," Tyler says, a little worried. "She's never gone this early even when she has to work." She should answer and he's becoming a little concerned. "Can you try her room number again, please?"

The desk clerk tries it again and again no answer. "Sorry, sir, still no answer."

Tyler goes to the nearest restaurant for a cup of coffee to give Sam a little more time thinking that maybe she was in the shower and didn't hear the phone. A few tourists are starting to stir and are showing up in the restaurant for an early breakfast or cup of coffee.

It's after eight and Tyler works his way back over to the front desk only to find a line of people waiting to check out. His patience is wearing thinner and he heads for the lounge. He decides to call George on his cell phone and have him call in and ask for Sam's room to see if they'll put him through. If he calls himself they'll recognize his voice.

If he has any luck George can get her room number and call him back.

When George answers the phone he automatically assumes Tyler's seen Samantha. "Tyler how's Samantha?"

"I wish I knew George!" Tyler replies.

"What the hell do you mean, you wish you knew? Aren't you with her?"

"Hell no, I'm not with her! I can't get the desk clerk to give me her room number and when they called her room she didn't answer! Now there are so many people standing in line to check out I'll never get up there. I want you to do me a favor."

"Anything, Tyler, you name it. But I don't know what I can do from here."

"I want you to call here and ask to speak to her. If I'm not mistaken they should connect you to her room. Then after you talk with her either have her come down to the lobby and meet me or call me on my cell phone." He gives George the number.

"That should work, I'll try. Give me a few minutes. If she doesn't agree to call you or come down I will call you back."

"I hope to hell it's her voice I hear and not yours! Thanks, George."

"You're welcome and hang in there!" George hangs up to call the hotel back.

George is immediately connected to Samantha's room and her phone is ringing, but there is no answer. Soon the hotel desk clerk comes on and says he's sorry, but no one is answering that line.

"Are you sure you have the right room? Can you please try it again for me?"

"I'm sure I punched the right room, but let me try it again." After trying, he comes on the line again without having any luck. "Sir, I'm sorry, no one is answering."

"Thanks for trying." George hangs up and dials Tyler's cell phone.

Tyler's cell phone rings and he recognizes the office number. "Wouldn't they put you through, George, or she wouldn't talk to me? Which is it?"

"Neither, Tyler. They tried her room twice, but, dammit, she didn't answer either time. What do you think?"

"I don't know what to think. Maybe she got up early and took a walk. Hell, I don't know. I think I'll hang around for a while and see if I run into her and if I don't I'll have someone from the front desk try her room again for me."

"I'll be here if you need me. Call as soon as you've caught up with her. I don't think I'll worry her parents just yet. She's probably just enjoying her stay and you're overreacting."

"She's being a pain in the ass. Why couldn't she just stay put? Women!"

Laughing on the other end of the line, George remarks, "Are you sure she's still worth the trouble, Tyler?"

"Huh, that's a mouthful. You know the answer to that one without even asking."

"Relax, I'll talk to you soon." He hangs up, shaking his head and sits back in his swivel chair. He's thinking to himself that Tyler's going to have his hands full when he catches up with Samantha and finds out she's thinking about relocating to Hawaii. He wasn't about to bring that subject up to him now. It'll all come out in due time.

Between the restaurant, pool area, beach, and lobby Tyler's exhausted the Marriott's grounds the entire day and still hasn't seen hide nor hair of Sam and he's getting extremely worried. If it takes another trip to the front desk then that's where he's headed.

Once at the front desk, there obviously was a shift change and he's hoping the gentleman now on duty is cooperative. "Sir, I'm very concerned about a young lady that checked in here a couple days ago."

"And you are?" the desk clerk asks.

"I'm Tyler Wentworth. I'm also registered here at your hotel." He gave him Samantha's name and told him the same information he gave the clerk earlier this morning.

"I'll ring her room and see if she's there. If she doesn't answer I'm afraid there's nothing more I can do either." Ringing Samantha's room there's no answer now, either. "Sir, I'm sorry, but there's no answer now, either."

Tyler's very upset and worried now. "Is there anyway we can go up and make sure she's okay?"

"No, we can't. Not without proper authorization."

Tyler's heard this before and he's ready for it this time. He's on his cell phone immediately to Mike at the hotel in Oahu who made the reservations here for Sam. Luckily when he's connected to the hotel he's told Mike is there but they need to locate him and he's put on hold.

"Mr. Wentworth, how can I help you?" Tyler hears when Mike comes on the line.

"Mike, I'm here at the Marriott where Samantha's staying. She doesn't know I'm here and the desk clerk obviously won't give me her room number. I've waited all day searching the entire resort and haven't seen her anywhere. It's not like Samantha to hole up in a room the entire day. She's on vacation for crying out loud. I'm getting very concerned that something's wrong. Can you help me?"

"How do you want me to help?"

"Can you call here and explain the situation and tell them I'm legit. I'm hoping they'll listen to you and maybe they'll let me go with them up to her room and see if she's okay."

"You do understand this is not customary, don't you?"

"Absolutely, and I wouldn't ask if I didn't feel there's something wrong."

"Go to the front desk and wait for me to call. I'll see what I can do, but I'm not making any promises. Even though I made her reservations there, I don't have any pull."

"I'll wait at the desk and I thank you. I appreciate your efforts." Tyler hangs up and heads for the front desk.

The desk clerk is already on the phone when he reaches the front desk and Tyler assumes he's talking with Mike because the desk clerk acknowledges Tyler when he sees him.

When the desk clerk hangs up he walks over to Tyler. "You are definitely persistent, aren't you?"

"Yes, I am. Is there anyway you can help me now?"

"Yes, there is. Mike confirmed you are who you say you are and what the circumstances are. Let me get my keys and confirm the room number and we'll head there.

"Thank you very much." He's hoping beyond all hope that she's fine, but his gut's telling him otherwise.

"I hope you're up for a little walk," the desk clerk remarks, coming out the door beside the front desk and meeting up with Tyler.

"Where are we walking to?"

"She's staying in a villa down by the ocean. It's located about a quarter of a mile down the beach from the main hotel."

"A villa! Well, how nice. I guess she's been living the life of luxury while she's here." He says this sarcastically.

"I've seen the villa's, but I haven't stayed in one myself. I can't afford them," the desk clerk replies.

Approaching Samantha's villa, Tyler's heart is starting to beat a little faster. He steps in front of the desk clerk before he gets to the door and starts knocking himself. But Samantha doesn't answer, so Tyler knocks louder and shouts her name. "Sam, are you in there?"

Again, he gets no response and he knocks again and, again, he hollers her name. This time, he thinks he hears something. "Did you hear that?" he asks the desk clerk.

"No, I didn't hear anything."

"Come closer." Tyler then once again asks if she's in there.

This time, both Tyler and the desk clerk hear her say something that sounds like help me.

"Open the damn door!" Tyler says to the desk clerk.

The desk clerk puts the key card in the door and the first time it doesn't work. Knowing Tyler is getting even more impatient, he tries again and this time the green light comes on and, turning the doorknob, the door opens.

Tyler practically knocks the desk clerk away getting inside, only to find Sam lying doubled over in bed, crying, "Help me."

"Sam, what's wrong?" Tyler knew something was wrong all along. He had bad vibes. She doesn't even know who's there or where she is. "Call 911, she needs medical help now. Sam, it's Tyler. Do you know who I am?" He gets no response again.

Emergency help is on its way, but as far as Tyler's concerned it's not soon enough. He's cradling Sam in his lap on the bed and the desk clerk is staying with them.

The ambulance arrives and is working on Sam to try to assess her condition, but without any help from her they don't know what's going on. They insert an IV and try to stabilize her and tell Tyler they need to get her to the hospital immediately. They're questioning him, but, unfortunately, he hasn't been there and is of no help to them.

The gurney arrives and Samantha's carefully lifted onto it. Tyler doesn't have a car to follow them and they okay it for him to ride up front in the ambulance. He thanks the desk clerk for his help and the ambulance is off with siren blaring. The desk clerk makes sure the villa is locked up before heading back to the front desk. It's been quite a different evening for him and he hopes she's going to be okay.

Upon arrival at the local hospital, Samantha is immediately taken to the emergency room and, of course, Tyler is not allowed in, but is asked to stop at the desk and give them all the necessary information on Sam. Luckily, he'd had his wits about him and picked up her purse off the dresser as he was leaving her hotel room.

Once he's supplied them with all the information he can he needs to contact George, so he can call her parents. He knows if any medical issues arise they will have to make the decisions, not him.

"I've been waiting for your call, Tyler. Is she there?"

"She's here, alright, but I have a bit of bad news." It's just now hitting him how serious this could be and he has to take a seat in the emergency waiting room.

"I had to call Mike back at the hotel in Oahu and he called the Marriott here to get them to let me in her room."

"She still didn't answer her phone?" George asks.

"No, she didn't, George. She couldn't."

"What do you mean, *she couldn't?*" Now George is getting a little concerned.

"George, I waited all day on her and canvassed this whole resort and never saw hide nor hair of her. I got very concerned. After Mike called and they tried Sam's room, rather villa, again I finally convinced them to take me to her villa and we'd try to raise her. When we got there we knocked on the door and there was no answer. We knocked again and I thought I heard a voice saying, *Help me.* The desk clerk didn't hear it, so we knocked again. After about the third time he heard her. He finally used the key card and unlocked the door. I rushed in and there she was, lying doubled over in a ball on the bed. She didn't even know who I was, George. We called 911 and they now have her in the emergency room, trying to figure out what's wrong with her."

"Good God, what could be wrong?"

"I don't know, but I hope they find something out soon. Would you please contact her parents? They're the only ones who will be able to make medical decisions for her and they may need to be made soon. I'm sure approval can be made over the phone, but I'd like for them to have some heads up notice. They are going to be quite concerned and I'm sure they're going to want to catch the first plane out of Palmetto to Maui and it isn't a short flight."

"I'll contact them immediately, but I think they will want to talk directly to you first. Is that alright with you?"

"Absolutely. I don't know anything at the moment, but I hope to hear something soon. I've given the hospital all the information about her I can, but as far as her medical background they'll have to give them that. I just hope and pray it isn't something serious."

"This is déjà vu all over again, Tyler. Just like when I let the two of you take off and go to the university to investigate Courtney's death."

"Yes, but this time it's not my fault. They can't blame me."

"You're right on this one. Maybe this will open their eyes about you and give you another chance."

"Let's hope so," Tyler says, but right now he just hopes that she pulls through this.

"I gotta go, Tyler and call her parents. Take care of her and call me the minute you know anything. I don't care what time of day it is, you hear?"

"I'll be waiting to hear from her parents and the minute I hear anything I'll let you know."

Chapter Twenty-Five

"George, we can't believe what you're telling us. This can't be happening to our daughter again." Curt is trying to console Marty as she's weeping uncontrollably in a chair at the kitchen table.

"I know how you must feel. Is there anything I can do to help?"

"No, you've already done everything you can. We need to call Tyler and see what if anything he can tell us and we need to get a flight out as soon as possible." Curt is already looking up airport phone numbers in the phone directory.

"We'll contact you as soon as we know something and thanks again for notifying us." Curt hangs up only to pick up the receiver to dial Tyler's cell phone number.

"Tyler, this is Curtis Summers. Have you heard how Samantha's doing?" he asks with his arm now around Marty's shoulders, both of them standing against the kitchen sink for support.

"Hi, Dr. Slater was just out and talked with me a few minutes ago. I'm sorry to say he didn't have anything good to report. He did say her temperature is way up, which concerns him because that means infection. They've drawn blood, but that will take a while for the results. He did ask me if she'd eaten anything that would have made her sick and I had to say I didn't know because I haven't been with her."

"Is she awake?" Curt asks, being coaxed by Marty to ask.

"No, she isn't. The doctor said she's still moaning and moving her head back and forth, but it's because her temperature is so high. They're trying everything to get it lowered before it gets to dangerous levels. Hopefully, the blood tests can tell them something."

"We need to get a flight out of here as soon as we can. Will you contact us if you talk to the doctor again?"

"Sure. I'll do so immediately. I only wish they'd let me be with her, but there's no way they're going to let me in there, especially if there's an infection. Wait, the doctor's coming out now. Maybe he'll want to speak to you."

"Dr. Slater, I have Samantha's father on the phone."

"Good," Dr. Slater replies. "I need to talk with him."

"Doctor, how's our daughter? Can you tell us what is wrong with her?" Curt asks, concerned.

"I'm afraid I can't. I'm very concerned about her temperature. We can't seem to get it stabilized. We're still waiting on the blood test but for the time being it still seems to be rising. How soon can you get here?"

"We're working on that now. We'll get there as soon as we can. In the meantime, will you permit Tyler to be with her?" They know that she would want him regardless of what they may have thought of him in the past.

"We'll have to wait on the blood tests and if we don't have to put her in isolation we'll let him in, otherwise he can't."

"Oh my God, can it be that serious?" Curt doesn't think it can be.

"I don't want to blow smoke here. Yes, it can. We'll just have to wait and see, but in the meantime I suggest you and your wife get here as soon as you can."

"We will. Thank you, Doctor. Will you put Tyler back on, please?"

Dr. Slater hands the phone to Tyler. "Curt, is there anything you want me to do until you get here?" Tyler asks after taking his phone back from Dr. Slater.

"Yes, there is. When or if Dr. Slater gives you the okay we want you to stay in the room with Samantha. We know that's what she would want. I'm sure you heard what he had to say and we don't want her to be alone."

"I promise you I won't let her be alone for a minute if they do indeed let me in. You know how much I love your daughter. She's going to be alright, she has to."

"Thanks, Tyler. We'll be there as soon as we can. Bye." Curt hangs up the phone and is on the phone with the airlines in seconds. They have a flight out within four hours, but they're going to have to pack fast. The airport is an hour's drive from Palmetto and it's already eleven p.m. Marty's already throwing things in their suitcase, trying to hold herself together, but it's not working. She's trying to see through her tears and the tears are getting their clothes wet. Curt comes up to help her, but finds that it's best if he just stays out of the way. They've never been to Hawaii and have always wanted to go, but this isn't the way they wished to see it.

They arrive at the airport with a little time to spare and are both anxious but tired. It's getting late, but they have a flight to catch. They're trying to figure out the time difference as they're checking in at the counter. Their baggage is checked and they're heading for their gate when Curt's cell phone rings.

"Hello," Curt says, holding his breath a little, wondering if it's the hospital with news on Samantha.

"Curt, it's George. Have you heard anything on Samantha?"

"George, it's you. We've just arrived at the airport and our luggage is checked in. We have about forty-five minutes before our flight leaves. We talked with Samantha's doctor before we left and he really didn't give us much to go on. Her temperature is still going up and he wants us there as soon as possible. Until they get the blood tests back they don't know much. We did ask if he'd let Tyler be with her until we get there and he said yes, if they don't have to put her in isolation."

"Isolation. What the hell for?" Now George is getting overly concerned, also.

"If it's an infection and they don't know what it is, it could be contagious."

"How the hell could she be contagious?" George asks, thinking Samantha can't be contagious.

"No one was with her to know what has caused this. We don't even know what she could have eaten. We might be able to find out what she's eaten at the hotel, but even that would take some work. But what about outside the hotel?"

"Oh my God, Curt. This can be serious."

"Yes, it can be. I need to go, George. I'll keep you posted. If I can't call I'll have Tyler keep in touch."

"Fine, thanks. Give Samantha my love. She's pretty special, you know." George is visibly shaken as he hangs up.

Chapter Twenty-Six

It's the middle of the night when Curt and Marty arrive at the hospital but Tyler is very grateful to see them.

Marty's mouth is already open the minute she spots Tyler. "What have you heard from the doctor Tyler? Is her temperature going down?"

Looking over her head in Curt's direction for some support he says. "I'm afraid not. Dr. Slater's checked on her several times and it hasn't come down, in fact it seems to be rising a little more. I can tell by his tone that he's very concerned."

"How about the blood tests?" Curt inquires hoping that at least they have come back and can give them some direction.

"Yes, they are back but haven't shown them anything concrete. He's wondering if she might have encephalitis."

"Encephalitis!" Marty exclaims. "That can be very serious. What makes him think it could be encephalitis?"

"Her high fever, nausea, vomiting, disorientation and confusion are just a few signs of encephalitis." Tyler only repeats what Dr. Slater pointed out to him earlier.

"But isn't it usually found in children?" Marty inquires.

"Yes, it does. But that doesn't mean it can't happen."

"Did Dr. Slater say what steps he's going to take next?" Curt asks Tyler, becoming concerned about time elements now.

"He's ordering an MRI as we speak. Hopefully, that will shed some more light on Samantha's condition."

The words no more than get out of Tyler's mouth and Dr. Slater's coming down the hall towards them. "Dr. Slater, glad you're here. I'd like you to meet Samantha's parents, Curt and Marty Summers."

Extending his hand Dr. Slater introduces himself. "I've just ordered an MRI for your daughter."

"Do you really think its encephalitis, Doctor?" Marty inquires.

"I'm not sure, but her symptoms and the blood test point in that direction. The MRI should show us more."

"What will you be looking for from the MRI?" Curt asks.

"The MRI will show us if there is any swelling, bleeding or other abnormalities of the brain."

"The brain!" Marty shouts. "Oh my God, Curt. Doctor, is our daughter going to be alright?"

"I sure hope so, Mrs. Summers. We don't know how long she'd been lying there ill."

"But it couldn't have been very long, Doctor, she just arrived on the island no more than a day or two ago," Tyler remarks.

"But we don't know how soon after she got here that she became ill. Let's not draw any unnecessary conclusions here. Let's wait and see what the MRI shows us. If you'll excuse me, I want to go back in and check on her."

"Doc, can we see her?" Curt asks before he can get away.

"She's in intensive care. You can't go in until we can pinpoint her infection, but there's a window and you can look through there. I'm sorry I can't let you in."

"Please," Marty begs. "We'll only stay a minute or two."

"If you go in you have to put on the scrubs, a hat, and gloves. Will you do that?" Dr. Slater asks.

"We'll do anything you ask. We'd like Tyler to go in with us."

"Okay, follow me and I'll have one of the nurses get you ready." They follow Dr. Slater to the nurses' station.

Marty, Curt and Tyler can't believe their eyes when they see Samantha lying helplessly on the hospital bed. Marty and Curt walk up to one side and Tyler takes the other and he immediately takes Samantha's hand. He can't actually feel her hand because he has rubber gloves on but just being there with her means the world to him. Tears are streaming down his face. Talking to her he tells her he's there but what's hard is he doesn't think she can hear him. He brushes her hair away from her forehead. He just wants to touch her.

Curt and Marty are on the other side and Marty's holding her hand with one of hers and rubbing her arm with the other as Curt stands behind Marty with his arm around her. None of them have seen anything so pitiful. This can't be their daughter lying here so helpless.

Minutes seem like seconds and the nurse is in to shoo them out. They're ready to perform the MRI on Sam.

Both Marty and Curt nor Tyler was able to sleep at all in the waiting room and it's nearly daybreak. It's been too long and they're still waiting to hear from Dr. Slater and the results of the MRI.

"Anyone want any coffee?" Tyler asks, standing, rubbing his eyes. "I've got to have some caffeine and I need to stretch my legs." They've drunk all the coffee in the waiting room and there aren't any packets left to make more so he's going to have to look elsewhere.

"No, but I'll take a diet Pepsi," Marty says, stretching her legs. She's starting to stiffen up and she gets up to loosen them up.

"I'll take coffee with sugar," Curt says as he's reaching in his back pocket for his wallet.

"I'll get it," Tyler says when he sees Curt reaching for his wallet.

As he heads for the elevator the elevator door opens and Dr. Slater steps off.

"Dr. Slater. Do you have news about Samantha?" Tyler asks walking towards him.

"I have. Do you have a few minutes? I'd like to talk with you and Samantha's parents."

Seeing the concerned look on the Doctor's face, Tyler instantly forgets the coffee run. "Sure, I'm with you." He turns around and walks side by side with him.

Curt sees Dr. Slater and Tyler head their way and grabs for Marty's hand. "Honey, Dr. Slater's coming this way with Tyler."

"I don't like the look on his face," Marty says.

"What look?" Curt asks.

"That look of concern."

There are more people in the waiting room than just the Summerses and Tyler, so Dr. Slater wants to take them to his office.

"Mr. and Mrs. Summers, if you'll follow me please, I think we can talk more privately in my office."

Once in Dr. Slater's office, he offers them to sit, closes the door and approaches his leather chair behind his desk.

Curt can't stand the suspense any longer. "Doctor, this can't be good news or you wouldn't have brought us here. What's wrong with our daughter?"

"I'm not going to beat around the bush here. We have the results of the MRI."

"And?" Curt asks, looking over at Tyler, who's sitting there with his hands folded on his lap, but can't tell he's holding his breath.

"It's what I expected, she has encephalitis."

"Oh my God!" Marty exclaims. "How bad is it?" She's absolutely stunned.

"There's quite a bit of swelling of the brain. More, in fact, that I expected."

"Do you think that's because she'd laid there so long before help came?" Marty asked, even more worried now.

"Could be, we don't know," Dr. Slater says, swiveling back and forth in his chair. He hates having to give parents this kind of diagnosis. He has a daughter about the same age as Samantha.

"What kind of treatment will you give her?" Tyler asks, his heart beating so fast he feels like it's going to jump out of his mouth.

"We can treat the brain swelling and we're starting her on it now."

"She can have a complete recovery, right?" Tyler asks, knowing he's heard what can happen with people with encephalitis.

"She can, yes, but I also have to prepare you for what can happen."

Not wanting to ask, but needing to know, Curt asks, "What's the worse case scenario, Doctor?"

"Curt!" Marty exclaims. "I don't even want to hear it."

"But, Marty, we have to prepare ourselves."

"In a small percentage of cases, swelling of the brain can lead to permanent brain damage, which could leave her with speech problems, memory loss, learning disabilities and, in very rare cases, even death."

"No, she can't die!" Marty is crying uncontrollably now.

"We're going to do everything we can for her, that I can assure you. We'll give the medication time to work then we'll take another MRI and see if the swelling's going down."

"How long will this take?" Tyler asks. He's full of questions and so worried about Sam.

"If the medication works, the swelling starts going down and she starts coming around it could be a matter of a few days. Then we should be able to determine if there's any damage such as I'd mentioned."

"Well, Doctor, you've thrown us for a loop. We in no way expected this. Can we be with her now?" Marty asks, feeling helpless for the first time in her life where her daughter is concerned. She thought she was helpless when Todd died, but this is much worse.

"Yes, you can, but don't overdo it. You two might go in and not for very long at a time and then why don't the two of you let Tyler spend some alone time with her? I think it will do her some good. Talk to her. Give her your love and support."

"Thank you, Doctor, we will." Curt extends his arm to shake Dr. Slater's hand.

"You know, all three of you can't be of any good to Samantha if you don't get some rest, yourselves. You all look exhausted. Why don't you stop in and see her, then get some sleep and come back in the morning?"

"Curt and Marty, would you mind? You've been up all night and flown all this way. Why don't you get some rest and I'll stay with Sam?" He's hoping like hell that they agree.

Looking at Marty, Curt agrees, but knows Marty will not. "Marty, he's right. Let's let him stay."

"But he's been up all night, too." Marty doesn't want to leave either.

"Yes, but he happens to be a lot younger than we are. Samantha's going to need all of us when she gets better, so we'd better take care of ourselves now."

"Okay, you win. We don't even have a place to stay."

Tyler has an idea, but doesn't know if the Summerses will go for it. "Do you think the Marriott will let you stay in Samantha's room until she's back?"

"We don't have a key," Curt explains.

"I don't think, under the circumstances, that should be a problem. I'll call them right now and see what they say." Tyler pulls his cell phone out of his pocket and hits redial on his phone for the Marriott. Once he's explained the situation to the desk clerk and has it confirmed by his boss, the only thing the Summerses have to do upon their arrival is show identification.

Tyler remembers that he brought Sam's purse and he tells Curt. "Curt, when you go see Sam you might find her key card in her purse."

"Thanks, I'll look. That will help us convince the hotel who we are."

Chapter Twenty-Seven

Tyler stands vigil over Sam's bedside for the entire next week taking turns with her parents. Dr. Slater tells them that the medication isn't working as well or as fast as he'd like but the swelling is receding some. He also tells them that his main concern now is the length of time the swelling is staying. He'll be very surprised if there isn't some degree of permanent damage, but he isn't ready to share that with them yet. Miracles do happen and he wants to wait.

Curt and Marty were okayed to stay in Samantha's villa and are there now while Tyler's taking his turn at the hospital. They're getting used to lounging out on the lanai and taking walks on the beach even though they feel guilty doing so while their daughter is lying in the hospital.

Tyler's left her side long enough to empty the warm water out of her drinking cup to fill it with more ice and fresh water when he thinks he hears her moan. Dropping the cup into the sink he returns to her bedside to see if he is just hearing things. Taking her hand he talks to her to see if she'll respond. "Sam it's me, Tyler. Can you hear me? Sam, can you hear me?" But he gets no response. Dear God he thinks his minds starting to play tricks on him, he so desperately wants her to respond. He doesn't know how much longer he can watch her lie here.

Standing over her for what must be the thousandth time he picks up a wet washcloth and moistens her lips. Without realizing it she lifts her hand as if to stop him from doing so.

Totally shocked Tyler asks softly, "Sam, can you hear me?" He focuses on her eyes to see if they open. He takes her hand in his. "Sam, if you can hear me, squeeze my hand." It isn't a fast movement, but he slightly feels her squeeze his hand and tears start down his cheeks. "Oh my God, Sam, you can hear me. Squeeze my hand again." And she does. He immediately pushes the button on her bed to alert the nurse's station.

The nurse comes in and asks if there's anything she can do. Tyler looks up at her with those eyes full of tears. "She squeezed my hand."

"Are you sure?" The nurse asks. "It could be a reflex, you know."

"I'm sure. Look."

The nurse is beside Tyler and he talks to her again. "Sam, squeeze my hand." She slowly squeezes his hand.

"I'll alert Dr. Slater. Shall I call her parents or do you want to do it?"

"I'll do it, thanks." He takes his cell phone out of his pocket.

When the phone rings in Samantha's villa both Curt and Marty are afraid to answer. It can only be news from the hospital and as of late it hasn't been all that great.

"Curt, you answer I'm afraid, too," Marty replies, looking at Curt, who's getting up off the chaise out on the lanai.

"Chicken," He says, slipping into his sandals before entering the villa. Once inside, he answers the ringing phone, recognizing the phone number.

"Curt! Sam just squeezed my hand!" he says excitedly and, at the same time, wiping the tears from his face.

"She did what?" Curt asks, not sure he heard Tyler correctly.

"You heard me right, she squeezed my hand."

"We'll be right over. Keep talking to her. Is Dr. Slater with you? Has he seen it?"

"No, not yet. The nurse just left to page him."

"Curt, what's going on?" Marty is quizzing him.

"Get your clothes on. Samantha just squeezed Tyler's hand."

"Is he sure?"

"Yes, he's sure. The nurse witnessed it, also." Giving her a hug, he feels that this may be the beginning of her recovery. He sure hopes to hell it is. He wants his daughter back.

They both are practically running when they reach ER. Tyler's still holding Samantha's hand when they walk in and Dr. Slater is standing over her.

"Mr. and Mrs. Summer's I've got some good news. Go ahead, Tyler." He nods for Tyler to go ahead and talk to Samantha.

"Sam, I'm here. If you can hear me squeeze my hand." Samantha ever so slightly squeezes Tyler's hand.

"Oh my God, Curt, look. She's doing it. She's squeezing Tyler's hand." Now all three of them are crying. "Samantha, it's Mom, can you hear me?"

"Honey, its Daddy. We're here. Can you hear me?" Both Curt and Marty are standing over their daughter now.

Samantha's eyelids start to flutter and she's squeezing Tyler's hand again.

"Say it again, Mr. Summers," Dr. Slater requests.

"Honey, it's Daddy. We're here. Can you hear me?"

Once again, Samantha's eyelids flutter, but this time her eyes open ever so slightly. "Dad-d-y," she says so lightly, Tyler can barely hear her.

"Did you hear her, Curt?"

Curt can't even reply, he's so overwrought with joy.

"Mom, I'm thirsty," she says, whispering.

"Honey, we'll get you a drink." Marty looks at the nurse who's just come into the room and she nods in response. "Samantha, can you open your eyes so you can see to take a drink?"

Slowly, Samantha tries to opens her eyes, but they quickly close again.

"Samantha, I'm Dr. Slater. Can you try to open your eyes again, please?" He waits to see if she responds.

She slowly opens her eyes and this time she opens them a little further and she recognizes Tyler. "Tyler?"

"Yes, honey, I'm here." He's ecstatic that she knows he's here and he, too, is overwrought with emotion.

"Do you still want a drink?" Marty asks.

"Yes," she says and this time her head moves from one side to the other. Marty places the straw close to her lips, so she can take a drink. Seeing she wants more, she lets her have it.

"I need to examine her," Dr. Slater comments.

Samantha is becoming more alert, but is still very weak and is becoming aware of her surroundings. "What am I doing in a hospital?"

"You've been very sick," Tyler says.

"I was in the villa," she says. "I was alone and got very sick. Mom, Dad, how did you get here?"

"One thing at a time. I need to examine you, Samantha, and you need to remain quiet. I think it best if the rest of you wait outside."

Tyler kisses her on the lips for the first time and tells her he'll be in as soon as the doctor finishes and her parents tell her the same.

It isn't long before Dr. Slater comes out and allows them to reenter Samantha's room, but before he lets them go back in he gives them their orders. "I can't tell you how close we came to losing her. I'll want to do some tests to see if there's any brain damage, but time will also tell us a lot. She's a very lucky young lady. You can go back in, but don't stay too long. She needs her rest and plenty of it. Please don't abuse it or I'll have to step in."

"Believe me, we won't," Curt replies. "We don't ever want her to go through this again.

Chapter Twenty-Eight

The doctor releases Samantha from the hospital at the end of the next week once he's sure all the test results are negative and some of her strength is back. She's agreed to stay on the island under the doctor's care for a while before she heads back to Palmetto. Curt and Marty agree to return to Palmetto only if Tyler will stay with her, which of course he does. Wild horses can't pull him away from her now. With her parents staying at the villa they haven't had any alone time.

Curt and Marty arrive at the airport and Tyler helps them with their luggage. Samantha wanted to make the trip but knew she needed not to even ask because she'd get turned down. Her strength is slowly returning and this short trip would have been more like an all day outing so she said her goodbyes at the villa.

Tyler goes with them until they reach their gate and he can't go any further without a ticket. He says his goodbyes once he's received his orders from them and he assures them he'll take the best of care of Samantha and he'll keep in touch daily.

On his way back from the airport Tyler sees a flower shop up ahead.

Getting into the center lane he puts his turn signal on to make a left hand turn. Parking the rental car he enters the flower shop and is greeted by a lovely young lady he assumes is the owner.

"May I help you?" she asks as she watches Tyler's eyes looking around the room eyeing all the different arrangements.

"I'm looking for something special," he says.

"I'm assuming this is for a special young lady."

"Yes, it is. She's only been out of the hospital a short while."

"Do you know what you're looking for?"

"No, I don't but that arrangement over there is nice," He says as he points to an arrangement of several different flowers in all different colors.

"Great choice. I just made that one up and it's very fresh. If you'd like I can wrap it up for you."

"Yes, please, I'll take it." He reaches in his back pocket for his wallet and extracts his credit card.

Making small talk while she wraps the bouquet she asks, "Are you a resident on the island or just vacationing?"

"That's a good question. I sort of came to rescue a friend of mine and while here she became extremely ill."

"I'm sorry to hear that. Did you get to rescue her?"

"I guess you could say that. She's out of the hospital now. I just put her parents on the plane and I'm headed back to the hotel now to take care of her. The doctor won't let her leave the island until she's a little stronger and I'm going to stay with her."

"Sounds like she's a lucky girl to me" she says, putting the finishing touches on the bow.

Tyler doesn't respond. He thanks the saleslady as he picks up the bouquet and heads out of the flower shop.

He has one more stop and it's a little liquor store right outside the hotel. He'd passed it several times in and out on his way back and forth to the hospital. In fact he's finding it pretty easy to maneuver his way around he's been this way so many times.

He knows Sam isn't supposed to have alcohol while on medication but he'll make sure she only has a sip or two.

Sam is sleeping when he enters the villa so he tiptoes over to the little fridge as not to wake her and puts the wine in. With the medication she's on she sleeps like a log and he's not surprised that she doesn't wake up when he comes in. He's trying to find a place to hide the bouquet in the small villa, but that's not so easy when he has an idea. It's evening and the sun will be going down soon so he decides to put it outside on the lanai. There's so much foliage out there she'll never see it. He just needs to make sure it's in the shade.

Looking at his watch he's calculating what time Curt and Marty will be landing in Palmetto. He has a surprise planned and he doesn't want them calling right in the middle of it. He has a lot of making up to do starting with literally throwing her out of his hospital room over a year ago. Whether it'll do any good or not he has to try and if eating crow is part of it then that's what he'll do.

Chapter Twenty-Nine

Tyler finishes everything to his liking before she awakens. When she gets up she seems to be feeling better and has some energy. "Have you heard from my parents yet?" she asks, stretching not considering they haven't even had time to get home yet.

"No, they haven't been gone long enough to get home. How are you feeling?"

"Pretty good. Each day I'm getting more of my strength back. I feel like a walk, will you go with me?"

"Sure, just give me a couple minutes," he says, looking around the room to make sure everything's in order for later even though it's hidden. He grabs his cell phone in case Curt and Marty call.

"Do you think we can go out for the evening?" Sam asks, opening the sliding glass door going out onto the lanai. "I'm hungry and ready for a nice meal, just the two of us."

This is working right into Tyler's hands. With the long nap she'd taken he thought she'd be weak when she woke up and would want her meal brought in. "Sure, if that's what you want. Glad to be rid of your parents?"

"Don't put it that way! I just want to spend some time alone with you."

"Does that mean you're starting to forgive me?"

"I forgave you a long time ago."

"You could have fooled me," he says as they walk slowly along the beach. He doesn't want to wear her out if he's taking her out for the evening. He takes her hand in his in hopes that she doesn't pull away, and she doesn't.

"I just about lost you again, you know."

"I know. But you've done everything you can not to let that happen haven't you?"

"Yes."

"Tyler, I don't want to go back," she says, stopping and turning to look at him.

"What do you mean you don't want to go back? Back where? To work or back home period?" He doesn't know what's she's talking about.

"Neither."

"You're telling me you don't want to return to Palmetto nor to work at *The Carolina Tribune*?"

"That's what I mean. I'm surprised George hasn't told you."

"What's George got to do with this?" Tyler asks, baffled.

"I called George and asked him what he thought of the idea?"

"You did what?"

"I called him and asked him what he thought of the idea."

"And just what did George tell you?"

"He said I'd been through too much and I needed some rest. He told me to think long and hard on it and in the end if it's what I want he'd see what he could do to help me out."

"After everything that's happened do you still want to stay here and be away from your parents and everyone you know?"

"Not everyone!"

"But you don't know anyone here!" he says, looking at her like she's lost her mind.

"What will you do? Where will you live?"

"I asked George if he'd talk to some of his associates here and see if he could help me find something."

"You've just about got this thing figured out don't you? Sam, it's going to take you quite a while to recover completely. Can you afford to stay here and pay these prices until you can find a job, let alone feel like going back to work?"

"To answer your first question yes, I've just about got it figured out. I wasn't planning on getting sick but I'm feeling better every day. I think I can afford to stay until I find a job and feel like going back to work especially if."

"Especially *if* what?" he asks, not having any idea what she's about to ask.

"I've done a lot of thinking and I want you to stay here with me."

"Stay here with you and *what*?" He can't believe she's asking this of him.

"Stay here with me and we can go into business together. Tyler we can start our own business here. We both love it here and you can't say you don't. I need a fresh start and I can't go back to Palmetto with all the sad memories. There's Jacob, Courtney and Todd. There's nothing there for me anymore."

"But what about your parents? They'll be devastated!"

"But they'll get used to it," she says, facing him with desperation in her eyes.

"Samantha, think about what you'd be doing to George. He'd be losing two good employees, that is if I decide to go with this crazy plan of yours."

"So you're calling it a crazy plan?" she asks. "Besides, you're just temporary help, supposedly to cover for me while I'm gone. But you went off half-cocked to run after me! Lee should easily step into my position."

"My God, Sam, you have all the answers, don't you?" He can't believe she's this set on doing this. "Will you give me some time to digest this?"

"Of course, I will. You have about twenty minutes. I'm just

176

kidding," she says, pulling him in closer to her.

He responds and actually pulls her closer to him and holds her tight. What he's not ready to tell her just yet is, he doesn't care where he lives as long as it's with her, but he's going to make her squirm for throwing him this curve. And pay dearly she will.

Releasing his hold he says. "Sam lets head back. Do you still want to go out this evening or would you rather order in?" He's hoping like hell that she decides she wants to stay in. Otherwise she's going to spoil his surprise.

"As much as I'd like to go out and get away from the villa, I think I'd better stay in. Maybe tomorrow we can go. Do you mind staying in?"

Relieved he says. "No, that's fine. I'll order for us as soon as we get back. We can eat out on the lanai and watch the sunset." His plan is going to work out perfectly.

Chapter Thirty

The doorbell rings and Tyler's there in two steps to open the door. The cart is wheeled in and he tells him to roll the cart out onto the lanai. Samantha is already resting on the chaise enjoying the evening sunset. She's changed into the sundress she purchased at the little shop on her walk the day she became ill.

"I think I'll slip into the restroom before we eat," she says to Tyler, getting up out of the chaise and slipping into her sandals that are beside the chaise.

Perfect, Tyler thinks to himself. He can now retrieve the bouquet of flowers he'd hidden in the foliage. Looking over the bouquet it made it just fine. He places it in the middle of the table and hurries into the room for the bottle of wine he has cooling in the little fridge. Grabbing the glasses on his way out he's had just enough time to arrange the table before he hears the bathroom door open and Sam comes walking out.

"What's all this?" she asks. "You've been busy while I was indisposed."

"Have a seat Sam. Let's eat shall we?" He pulls her chair out for her and she sits down. He sits down also and they start uncovering the dishes that were brought in. Everything looks great and plated as Tyler requested. "Sam, you've never asked me why I'm here in Maui. I know you've been sick and your parents were here but have you ever wondered?"

"Yes, I did when I was in the hospital, but I haven't given it much thought since. Just why did you come to Maui?"

"Remember the incredible evening we had the evening before you flew out of here and left me stranded?"

"Yes," she says, thinking how could she forget it.

"Then why did you just take off like that?" he asks, cutting a piece of his steak.

"I was afraid," she says, looking up at him.

"Afraid of what for God's sake?"

"Dear God Tyler don't you know?"

"Know What?"

"I've had so many relationships go bad in two years I couldn't do it again! Couldn't you see that? And you were one of them! You broke my heart!"

"I know that. But you didn't have to take off like that. We were all worried about you. I couldn't find you so I called George and he contacted your parents. But I thought you'd gone to Colorado."

"Colorado! Why would I go to Colorado? It's freezing out there."

"Well, that's where I went. I flew to Scott and Tracie's only to find you weren't there and I spent the night."

"Oh my God, you didn't." She's laughing now. "How are they?"

"Who?" He's not seeing anything funny about it at all.

"Scott and Tracie."

"They're fine. Once I told them the whole story they couldn't believe what you'd done. They're a very nice couple by the way."

"Then how did you end up here?" she asks, taking a bite of a roll.

"I called George and he in turn called your parents to tell them you weren't there. They called the hotel in Oahu and finally convinced the hotel manager to tell them where you went. I then flew from Colorado to here only to find out that they wouldn't share your room number with me."

Sam can tell that Tyler's getting a little irritated reliving the experience. "That's enough, the rest is history. I'm just glad you're here with me now."

"Oh, you are, are you? That's easy for you to say, you don't know how furious I was with you. I felt like an idiot on Scott and Tracie's front porch looking for you and you weren't there. But nothing could have been as bad as finding you on that bed in the shape you were in. Dear God, I thought I was going to lose you all over again."

"I'm right here and I'm getting stronger every day." She reaches over to take his hand in hers. "I want to thank you for taking such good care of me and it hasn't gone unnoticed, Tyler," she says, rubbing her fingers over the top of his hand.

Calming down, he's thinking to himself, she's going to make this much easier for me. Faking a cough, he pushes his chair back and excuses himself from the table. Walking into the villa, he retrieves a little box from the dresser and returns to the lanai. Sitting back down, Sam doesn't see the little box because he has it sort of covered with his cloth napkin.

Samantha continues to eat and hasn't paid any attention to what he's doing. She just thinks he's trying to get his cough under control.

"Sam, do you believe in second chances?" he asks, taking her hand back in his and as he does she stops eating and looks up at him.

"Second chances at what?" she asks, still not having a clue what he's up to.

"I let you go once, Sam, but I have no intentions of letting you go again. I've had to live with myself ever since I saw the look on your face the day I sent you away at the hospital. You have no idea what that did to me that day. You didn't see me the day you married Todd, Sam. But I saw you from the back of the church. You and Todd were turning to walk back up the aisle. I saw the love in your eyes that day and I turned and left."

"You were at my wedding? Why didn't you stay?" she asks, so overwhelmed she can't believe she's hearing this.

"I actually came to stop the wedding, but I couldn't. When I saw you, I had to let you go. I knew you still loved me, you told me that. But you also told me you weren't in love with me anymore. Then when I saw the love in your eyes that you had for Todd I couldn't do it."

"And then you were there for me when he died. You were at his funeral."

"Yes, I was."

"You were here for me when I screwed up and thought I'd have a fling with someone I'd just met on the damn plane." She's beginning to see the whole picture.

"Yep," he says and she's stealing his thunder right out from in under him.

"And I almost died. I've been a complete fool, haven't I?" The man who really loves her is sitting right here in front of her.

"Will you shut up long enough for me to talk?"

"Yes."

"You did what you had to do after I sent you away. You went on with your life and you found Todd. That's what I thought I wanted you to do, but it wasn't. I kept in constant contact with George. He let me know when you started seeing Todd. He didn't like it a little bit that I was so stubborn. He kept telling me that I should come after you and I wouldn't. He said that you would up and marry him and I'd lose out and that's exactly what happened. But I thought you hated me and I didn't deserve a second chance."

"And now?" Samantha can hardly breathe.

Reaching into his pocket he brings out the box and opens it. "Sam I've loved you since I came to Palmetto to help you find Courtney's murderer and I think you know that. Yes, we've had our ups and downs, but if you remember we've also had some terrific times. I don't want to go another day without you, whether we're here in Maui, Oahu or back in Palmetto. Will you marry me?"

Tears streaming down her face, Sam couldn't be happier. She's finally getting the man she's loved since they first made love on their family boat over the fourth of July back in Palmetto. "Yes, Tyler, I'll marry you." Then she's speechless as she watches Tyler take the ring out of the box to place it on her finger.

Taking the platinum diamond solitaire out of the box he puts the ring on Sam's finger. Nothing has felt so good in his entire life. Getting up he walks around the table to pull her up from her chair and taking her in his arms kisses her. The kiss deepens into the passion that the two of them have waited what seems a lifetime for. Releasing her only slightly to move into the villa Sam follows him in. Once inside beside the bed Sam is facing Tyler. She doesn't know it but the new sundress she's worn on purpose hasn't gone unnoticed. He unties one strap at a time and lets them fall off her shoulders as she's looking into his eyes. Turning her around he unzips the dress and it falls to the floor at her bare feet as he lifts her hair to plant a kiss on her neck then unfastens her bra.

Turning her around he wants to see her when he lets the straps of her bra slide down her arms. In one motion he picks her up and lays her on the beautiful made bed of soft pastel cottons. He hasn't forgotten one inch of her body and can't get undressed fast enough. Lying in bed beside her he pulls her soft, mostly naked body as close to his as he can.

"Sam," he says, sliding his fingers to remove her bikini and feeling the heat.

"Hm?"

"Are you sure?" he asks, his warm hands exploring.

"Never more sure of anything in my life," she says, rolling towards him and opening herself to what they've both waited too long for.

Printed in the United States
58592LVS00006B/22-45

9 781424 118373